Jack's tone turned husky and sent a thrill down Freddi's spine. She was ultra aware of how sexily she was dressed. With his eyes on her, she felt exposed, vulnerable.

'I approve of the get-up.' His gaze was hot on hers. 'Why can't you wear those kinds of clothes all the time?'

'They'd be a bit restricting in bed.' Oh, hell, had she really said that?

His eyes smouldered. 'Are you a woman who likes a challenge?'

'Of course I am,' she said, trying to regain some ground. 'Otherwise I wouldn't be working for you.'

'Good.' He winked at her. How she wished he wouldn't do that. It caused instant meltdown. 'Want to arm wrestle?'

Was he joking? She bit her lip, eyeing the bulging width of his biceps. She could think of better things to do.

'What are the stakes?' she asked suspiciously.

His smile was sensual, suggestive and enough to have every lustful cell in her body come to quivering life.

'Don't worry. If you're lucky I might let you keep some of those sexy clothes on.'

Dear Reader,

I was flipping through the pages of a magazine when I came across an article that recounted one woman's experience at a school for butlers. What really caught my eye, though, was the photograph of her bringing breakfast in bed to her gorgeous hunk of an employer. Well! That was all it took to set the creative juices flowing.

Soon I was writing about the adventures of Freddi and Jack. Every now and then my husband appeared in my study to find out what was making me chuckle. Even our Himalayan cat, Figaro (the vainest cat in North America and a substitute for our four grown kids), nosed around my keyboard to sniff out what was keeping me so entertained.

I hope Freddi and Jack's romance will give you a smile or two, and reaffirm the importance of love. Spinning stories such as this allows me to share the passion, laughter and joy that I'm able to find in my life. Romance novels have helped me through the light and the dark moments of my many journeys and I hope this story can do the same for you.

Wishing you as much fun in reading this as I had in writing it!

Brenda Hammond

Want to know more about Brenda Hammond? Visit eHarlequin at www.eHarlequin.com/authors.

AT YOUR SERVICE, JACK

by

Brenda Hammond

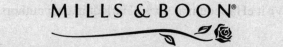
MILLS & BOON®

To Nancy Frost and Eve Silver.
Working with you is right up there with the best
things that have ever happened to me.

*First published in Great Britain 2003
by Harlequin Mills & Boon Limited,
Eton House, 18-24 Paradise Road, Richmond, Surrey TW9 1SR*

© Brenda Hammond 2002

ISBN 0 263 83571 5

21-0903

*Printed and bound in Spain
by Litografia Rosés S.A., Barcelona*

1

FREDERICA IMOGEN ELLIOTT negotiated the icy steps leading up to the oak-paneled front door, a flight bag dangling from one hand. Her fancy, lizard-skin boots were definitely not up to keeping a grip on Toronto's pavements in March. The leather soles slithered and slipped all over the place. And she didn't appreciate the fast-flying snow that seemed determined to blanket her. Thank goodness her stiff-brimmed hat kept the flakes out of her eyes.

At the top, her gaze met the eye-level, brassy glare of the door knocker—a lion with an overbite problem. Seizing the ring, she gave it three sharp raps. Her satisfaction evaporated when she noticed a bell on the left. Why couldn't she get anything right?

Seconds before she was transformed into a snow-woman, a man with a tattoo and a day's growth of beard yanked open the door. Oh God, Freddi thought, what had she got herself into? He was so tall. And his clothes! There was no hemming at the neck of his T-shirt, which meant she could see his chest. His sweatpants hung loose and low at the waist, revealing a slice of taut, lightly furred stomach. What a scruff. And he was wearing a bandanna! Her first, and with any luck, only, assignment was going to be much more difficult than she'd ever imagined.

She cleared her suddenly husky throat. "Good evening, Mr. Carlisle. I'm Freddi Elliott and—"

"Sorry, I'm not entertaining till later." His voice was gruff, his consonants slurred. And he shut the door in her face.

How rude! This man was definitely in need of civilizing. If she wasn't so desperate to fix her life she'd turn around right now and go back to the U.K. Trying not to feel intimidated, Freddi jabbed the bell. Again the door opened.

Dark eyebrows crunched together. "I told you to go away!"

Quickly, before he could close the door, she shoved her foot into the narrowing gap.

"Just a minute!" Her voice rose horribly close to a squeal. "You're expecting me."

"I am?" The door opened a fraction wider. "You must be mistaken." He folded his arms across the not-to-be-ignored width of his chest. "I know that the woman I'm expecting tonight is tall and blond, just as I specified. Obviously, you don't fit the bill."

Quickly he looked her up and down, one eyebrow quirking when he saw her footwear. "Quite apart from the fact that—" unfolding his arms, he shot his wrist forward and checked his watch "—if you *are* the babe from the agency, you're an hour early."

Jet lag must have affected her ears, because it simply wasn't possible that she'd heard him correctly.

"I thought I was precisely on time," Freddi protested. "And what difference would my height or the color of my hair make?"

He smiled, a slow, sizzling smile, "Blond hair and long legs are guaranteed to turn me on. So now—" he gripped the doorjamb "—you can remove your foot and its reptilian casing."

Blinking at him, she did as he asked. He promptly stepped back and shut the door.

She stared at the unyielding barrier. Life seemed determined to hand her yet another obstacle, not satisfied with the fact that she was broke, carless and homeless. In spite of the hollow feeling that was spreading through her, she couldn't give up. Mustering her courage, she leaned on the bell again.

After four seconds her new employer reappeared. "What *is* your problem, lady?" His frown was fearsome to behold.

"*My* problem?" In agitation she began to swing her carry-on bag backward and forward. "There must be a misunderstanding here."

"You misunderstood when I told you to get lost?" His glance flicked down to the purse/pendulum and he took a step back, as if worried that she would hit him in the crown jewels.

"No." She swallowed. "But are you really sure that's what you want?" Stilling the bag, she stuck her aristocratic nose in the air. "My idea—" she said in her snottiest tone "—is that your butler is *not* supposed to turn you on."

The man goggled at her.

She gave a sniff, determined not to succumb to tears. "Maybe I'll just climb back into the taxi and return to the airport."

"Did you say *butler?*"

"Yes." She stared back at him, beginning to get annoyed. Even if she usually managed to remain cool and dignified, this combination of circumstances was rather daunting. Her years of secretarial work had gone smoothly, predictably. But her salary had hardly been enough to keep a racehorse fed, let alone pay for the sky-high Visa bill her ex-fiancé, Simon, had saddled her with. His sister Tabitha, her friend who owned the buttling agency, had convinced Freddi to take this job, saying it would solve all her financial problems and set her on track again. Because of her upbringing, Freddi knew exactly what a butler should do. She could easily wing it, and Mr. Jack Carlisle would be none the wiser.

Freddi took a small step closer to him. "As you didn't hear the first time, I'll repeat. I'm Elliott, your butler, you... If you intend to send me away, then the least you can do is give me some money to pay the driver. I don't think he'll accept my Visa." Not that it would do any good if he did, she thought.

Maybe the man didn't understand English too well, because instead of responding, he just stood there, arms folded, biceps bulging, staring at her out of hazel eyes. She clutched at the strap of her bag. This was going from bad to worse. She'd just about called Mr. Jack Carlisle an idiot. Not the best way to impress her new employer. The dreaded jet lag must have exaggerated that impetuous streak she'd been working so hard to eliminate, making her forget that she really needed this job.

So much for the warm welcome she'd been expecting. While snow accumulated on her shoulders, her courage dwindled. Yet another undisclosed, pernicious side effect of air travel. Clearly Mr. Carlisle was far too obtuse, far too crass for her to live with for the next three months. Bad enough to have to perform the role of butler at all. She'd only given in to Tabby's urgings because she was desperate for a way out of her difficulties. But to perform such a role for Jack Carlisle would be impossible.

Freddi turned on her heel, thinking she'd better cut her losses and leave. She took two and a half tottering steps before Mr. Obnoxious called out.

"Wait!"

At that moment her serpent boots decided she should take a shortcut. Her heels slid out from under her and she found herself dumped on her rear end, gliding downward. Visions of lying in a pathetic heap at the bottom of the stairs were suddenly preempted. Jack leaned out and grabbed her arm, saving her from a slippery fate. The man had quick reflexes, she'd grant him that, even if he was slow on the uptake. Through the thick wool of her Jaeger coat she could feel the strength of his grip.

He hauled her upright with one large, firm hand, and continued to hold her, his gaze steady. "Just a minute. I'm starting to get the picture here. You said you're Freddi who?"

"Freddi Elliott, your new butler—presuming you are Mr. Jack Carlisle—"

Jack didn't say anything.

"But I've decided to quit before I begin," she muttered, doing her best to sound aloof, an effect which she could achieve rather well.

"Let me get this straight," he began.

A mild bout of dizziness hit her and she swayed, closing her eyes. His grip tightened.

"You're Elliott, my butler, right? The agency sent you."

Eyes open again, she looked up at him. "Both statements are one hundred percent correct."

"But you're not supposed to be a woman!"

She raised her eyebrows and closed her lids in a gesture that used to drive her younger brother crazy. Then, putting on her best expression of disdain, she looked down at the fingers curled around her upper arm. They sent strange sensations dancing across her skin.

"You'd better not be discriminating against my gender," she warned, latching on to one last hope. "That's illegal." Her words were beginning to slur and she felt light-headed. The combination of extreme fatigue and jet lag was taking its toll.

He pulled her toward the door. "You'd better come inside. We can't sort this out here."

In spite of the freezing weather, Jack Carlisle wore a sleeveless T-shirt and his feet were bare. When he at last allowed her into the narrow, three-story house, Freddi understood why. Compared with the icy confines of her family's baronial mansion, which cost far more to heat than her father could afford, Jack's home was kept tropically warm.

Freddi followed him from the small, slate-floored entrance hall up three steps and into a large open space, one section of which held a long, dark oak table. He skirted the open stairwell with its spiral staircase, passed the dining section and flopped down onto a large, low easy chair. In front of this sat a matching ottoman. Jack put his bare feet up and crossed them at the ankles, regarding her with an enigmatic expression.

Her new employer had not suggested she remove

her hat or coat, and now he neglected to invite her to sit down. Mr. Carlisle was definitely in urgent need of tuition in the normal politesse of everyday life. He didn't even seem to care that it was rude to stare. At any other time, as part of her expanded job description, she would have tactfully pointed out these lapses.

Feeling self-conscious in the focus of Jack's gaze, she dropped onto one corner of the six-foot-long black leather couch and sank gratefully into its soft and comfortable embrace. She would ignore him. But when she lowered her eyes, she found herself staring at his feet. Silence fell, broken only by the occasional hiss and crackle of the logs burning cozily in the open fireplace. To her relief, Jack got up and walked over to the curved corner bar.

Soon the warmth, the gradual relaxation of her tense mood and equally tense muscles began to make her sleepy. Maybe, if she hadn't been so exhausted it would never have happened. Whatever, she could feel her eyelids growing heavier and heavier until she no longer had the will to prevent them from closing.

Meanwhile, Jack stood leaning on the corner bar. He drummed his fingers on the glass top. From the row of glasses arrayed on the shelf above, he selected a heavy-based tumbler. He unscrewed the top off a bottle of whiskey, poured himself a decent shot, then grabbed a couple of ice blocks from the small bar fridge. Lifting the glass in a toast to himself, he took a sip. The distinctive, woodsy taste filled his mouth, and slid in a fiery stream down his throat. What a situation. This was not at all what he'd been expecting.

His cousin, Tabitha James, had started the ball rolling. On the phone, he'd told her about needing more capital.

"What for?" she asked.

"There's this new method of bonding metals that I've discovered. I have to develop further applications for it."

"What happened to your other investors?"

"Everyone's skittish because of the downturn in the economy."

"Have you approached Uncle Avery?"

"Sure." Jack sighed. "But the old fart says he's got reservations. He's holding off on final approval."

Apparently Simon, Tabitha's brother, had voiced his own biased opinion of Jack's lack of proper manners, uncultivated ways and inability to settle down. He'd reminded Uncle Avery of that fiasco when Jack was twenty-three, freshly graduated from college. The time he accidentally hit the prime minister on the back of the head with an escargot.

Simon had their uncle's ear. Not only was he on the spot, but recently he'd been appointed international marketing manager for the family corporation, which manufactured hard-rock mining machinery and equipment. Uncle Avery would visit soon to check up for himself, and in the meantime had advised Jack to find a suitable woman of good breeding. The right spouse was a tremendous advantage in life. So it was vital to Jack's future that he play along with old Avery, get someone to help smarten him up, coach him in etiquette and bring an element of class and organization into his life. Otherwise, he could kiss any chance of money goodbye.

That was when Tabby had suggested he hire a butler, a person who would know all about manners, and could take some of the pressure off his ultrabusy life. Generally, keep him in line. If he paid a higher fee, both roles could be combined, and she had just the right candidate.

After mulling over the idea, he'd decided to go for it. His mind went back to the closing dialogue of that fateful phone call.

"There's only one person available, Jack. The only snag—"

"Great. Just e-mail me the details—employment conditions, name and time and date of arrival."

"I just want to mention one thing—"

"No, no. If you have someone who fits the bill, I'm happy."

"Are you positive, Jack?" Tabitha had asked.

"Sure I am."

"Right. Then I'll fax the contract over for you to sign."

Now he understood the unmentioned detail, the snag, the meaning of that one thing. The man who would help ensure his future was a *woman*. And Tabitha, when she had faxed the contract, had spelled the name "Freddy," leading him to believe his butler was male.

He supposed it *might* be polite to offer her a drink, seeing as she hadn't yet officially assumed her duties. He scratched up a handful of peanuts from another small dish he'd set out on the frosted-glass bar counter in anticipation of company coming, and chewed on them.

The other part of Uncle Avery's stipulations had also caused problems finding a proper woman. Because of

working more than full-time for Quaxel, the branch of
the family corporation that his father had founded in
Canada, as well as putting in hours on his own inno-
vative product at night, Jack was out of circulation.
During university days he'd played the field, but
shortly after, settled into a relationship that had lasted
for three years, until Clare was offered a job on the
West Coast. By then they had both realized that, while
they were comfortable with each other, there was no
passion in their relationship.

His sister had fixed him up with a few of her friends,
and the results had been awkward and embarrassing.

Eventually, he'd decided to consult the experts.
That's what his dad had always done. So Jack contacted the most exclusive dating agency in town, and
was hoping they'd come up with a woman who could
please both him and Uncle Avery. Number one, the
pick of the crop, was due to arrive at any minute.

Strange that Ms. Elliott hadn't said anything since
she'd sat down. She'd been mouthy enough before
that.

Jack turned to her and asked, "How soon could you
leave, do—"

He broke off. It was obvious he wasn't going to get
an answer. Freddi had keeled over sideways on his
couch. Her Mad Hatter's tea party hat had fallen off
and was now settled neatly in the center of the Persian
carpet. Its owner lay dead to the world. Either she'd
drunk too much on the plane or she was flat-out
exhausted.

Gingerly, Jack crept toward the couch and stood
looking down at her. Why hadn't he seized the opportunity when she'd offered it and sent her right back

where she came from? But she'd looked so pathetic
standing there in that ridiculous hat, all pale face and
large chocolate-brown eyes. Now what was he supposed to do? Lying curled up on his couch she seemed
vulnerable, yet somehow trusting. Little did poor Ms.
Freddi Elliott know that she'd stepped right into the
lion's den.

2

THE BELL CHIMED. Jack went to open the front door and found a man in uniform, standing on the top step.

"Sorry, mister. I can't wait any longer," implored the limo driver.

"She asked you to wait?"

"Yeah, but there's cars backed up behind me, and one of the drivers is threatening to call the police." The man brushed at his cap, looking at him as if he was nuts not to have noticed. "Didn't you hear the honking?"

"No." Leaning forward, Jack stretched his neck out and saw the limo double-parked, blocking the narrow side street. Stuck behind a black BMW, a cheeky blue Beetle flashed its headlights at him.

"Okay. Let me pay you and then you can go. How much?"

He named his price. Jack shoved a hand into the back pocket of his sweatpants and drew out his wallet. He added a good tip.

"Thank you very much." The driver folded the bills. "I put the bags on the sidewalk."

"Cool. I'll come down and get them."

Jack slid his feet into his running shoes. He heard the limo's trunk slam closed and revving noises as the line of cars moved off.

Outside, the sidewalk had taken on the appearance

of garbage day. Near the base of a slim, bare maple tree waited a suitcase nearly as big as his refrigerator. Next to that were huddled two other shapeless bundles. It looked as if Freddi Elliott intended to stay for a very long time.

He gripped the handle of the suitcase and lifted. What on earth? Was the woman smuggling gold bricks? No way was he going to haul this lot up to the room on the second floor. He'd already done a punishing session with weights at the gym earlier. Better to leave the whole pile in the entrance, handy for the morning. It was enough that he had to decide what to do with her.

Casting a glance toward Freddi, Jack retrieved his drink and sat down again. She looked pretty comfortable lying there, one small hand tucked under her pale cheek, a stray lock of almost-black hair caressing her forehead. He'd never seen a hairstyle quite like that. It looked as if someone had chopped off random chunks with the shearing scissors. The effect might be appealing, but she was as far away from his notion of Jeeves as it was possible to get.

What to do? He had definitely hired a butler, one F. I. Elliott. If only he could unhire her immediately and get a replacement. But he'd signed the contract. His only option was to make things impossible for her so that she'd quit.

The doorbell rang. Jack leaped to his feet. The first of his dates had arrived! With any luck he was about to remedy the sexual famine of the last while. And then he remembered the snag on the couch.

Impossible to make any moves with Elliott sleeping

by the fire. She'd put a definite crimp in his plans for
the evening. He'd have to get her upstairs. Pronto.

Stooping down, he edged his hands under her
shoulders and hips, and heaved her up. She was a lot
heavier than she looked. Maybe she had the muscle to
carry a loaded tray after all. Unbidden, an image of the
waif dressed up as a French maid, flitting around his
living room, popped into his mind. Stop it, Jack. Already he felt she was intruding on him.

He managed to get her halfway up the curving staircase when the doorbell rang again. He froze. Damn.
But he couldn't just drop his burden and head back
down again. The blonde would have to wait.

Jack carried Freddi past the door leading to his own
room and into the next one. He'd had the guest room
specially decorated for a butler, all in masculine beiges
and browns. The designer had said a Brit would surely
appreciate living in various shades of tea.

Freddi showed no signs of waking, not even when
he tugged those ridiculous boots off her feet. She was
as floppy as a black nylon stocking. Thoroughly distracted, he came to the conclusion there was only one
other person he knew who slept as soundly as she did,
and that was the magnificent, muscular and intelligent
Mr. Jack Carlisle.

The doorbell rang yet again.

He was about to answer it when he paused. Surely
he needed to cover her. Her coat would have to do for
now—he had no time to fumble with the duvet. He
grabbed an arm and began to tug at the sleeve. If he
maneuvered her a little to one side, lifted up her spine,
then he'd be able to pull the coat out from under her.
He remembered seeing his sister do that to her kid

once. The only difference, as Jack found soon enough, was that little Kim didn't have boobs and Freddi most definitely did. As he lifted her, she arched her back. He froze. Not five inches below his chin the outline of her breasts showed clearly beneath her thin, clingy sweater. How easy it would be to lower his head... Dammit, he was as horny as a rabbit! Never mind the duvet, he had to get out of there, fast.

DOWNSTAIRS, he was making his way to the front door when he tripped over Freddi's hat. He cursed, picked it up and hurried to the door, hoping the lady wasn't too vexed. But when he opened it he saw nothing but swirling snow. He swore in frustration.

He gave a quick glance up and down Acorn Street, then shut the door again. He twirled the hat on his fingers and plonked it on top of her luggage. Seeing as his date had disappeared, he'd better cancel his dinner reservation. He decided to order a good-size pizza.

A little while later he sat munching and thinking. He had to find a way to get rid of Elliott. Already she was causing trouble. Leaning back in his chair, he let his mind float. He thought about his sister Louise, and Kimmie, his niece. The last time he'd baby-sat he'd read her a bedtime story, a neat fairy tale where the hero was given three tasks to accomplish.

Bingo. He sat up straight. That was his answer. He'd set Elliott three impossible tasks and she'd surely get the message and quit.

Now all he had to do was scheme them up.

Soon inspiration struck. Jack had an idea for the first impossible task. Definitely he himself would find this extremely taxing, and he imagined that, given the state of his kitchen, Elliott would too. With a grin, he bounded up the stairs to his third-floor office. After booting up his computer and opening a new document, he stared at the blank screen. A quick nod, a chuckle, and he began composing his note.

In Jeeves's room he found Freddi lying just as he'd left her.

He pried his gaze away from her sleeping form. Now, where to put the note so that she saw it when she woke? On top of the mahogany chest of drawers was the obvious place. Surely the bright-yellow paper would catch her eye. Propping it against a photograph of the Tower of London—the designer had insisted it would make Jeeves feel at home—Jack decided it would be interesting to see how Elliott would react to his somewhat insolent demand.

IN HER OLD-FASHIONED, Hampstead flat the bathroom was just across the hall from the bedroom. So, when groggy Freddi got up from the bed in Toronto, she opened the door and stumbled across the passage. There she found the bathroom. Confused to discover she was still in her clothes, she undressed and cast them onto the floor. After flushing, she groped her way back. Her fingers encountered the smooth stainless knob. Silly that she'd shut the door behind her. She tottered forward into the darkness and slid back into bed.

Minutes later, a pleasant sensation caused her to rise gradually out of Morpheus's realm. Vaguely she became aware of a warm, male body shifting in behind her. She snuggled closer. One heavy hand crept over her waist, seeking fingers curled around her breast. A certain vital piece of male anatomy stirred. And grew.

Languorously, she stretched her legs down and turned toward the lure of love, her body already heating, becoming fluid. Lifting her arms, she wound them around the firm muscles of the man in the bed and pressed closer. He responded by nibbling gently at her, the soft movements setting off tingling jolts of electricity. When the thrills began to turn her body to fire, she reacted by surging upward. She freed her hands to hold the firm jaw, and devoured his mouth with a deep and hungry kiss. God, did he taste good. This was like putting your tongue to the finest chocolate truffle. The outside was soft, silky. The inside more textured, more tasty, more explosive. And he felt like Adonis. She wanted more, and he was willing to cooperate.

When at last the kiss ended, Freddi breathed out a long breath. This was bliss. This was searing and exciting. The only trouble was, this wasn't a dream, it was real!

Her eyes popped open. Her breathing stopped. The man half under her didn't smell familiar. Just to make sure, she turned her nose toward the ceiling and sniffed—a touch of wood smoke, a whiff of whiskey and something else—oh God—eau de Carlisle. Full realization hit. She was cuddling in bed with a stranger. *Her boss.*

She lay transfixed, her eyes wide and staring into the darkness. Even though she could feel the hardness pressing against her thigh, she thought just maybe Mr. Carlisle was still more asleep than awake. Quietening her own breathing, she listened. Was he conscious, or not? From the regular rhythm, she thought not. Which meant she might just have a chance to slip away.

Gingerly she slid one leg outward. No echoing shift

came from Jack. The other leg joined it. She was about to gather her forces and scamper off, when a strong arm grabbed her middle, rolled her over and crushed her back into a warm and ardent embrace. For three seconds she luxuriated in the potent sensation, her body unable to resist. But then her brain insisted she beat an immediate retreat. Making herself as slim as she could, she ducked down, slithered to the edge of the bed and rolled out. Ignoring Jack's mutters of displeasure, she crawled, full speed ahead, to the exit. When she was safely out in the passage again, she stood up, closed the door so quietly there was hardly a whisper as it settled into its frame, and got herself into the adjacent room.

Shaken, disoriented, she closed herself in and stood leaning back, staring into the darkness. Where had that libidinous woman come from? How she'd got to bed was a mystery. How she'd got herself to the bathroom, she didn't know. But now, to reassert her grasp on reality, she needed to see where she was. Running her hand over the wall, she found the light switch.

Slowly, she considered the room. Apart from her coat, it was empty of her belongings. Then she spotted the bright-yellow note.

Freddi tiptoed across to the chest, snatched up the piece of paper and read:

Elliott—I expect breakfast in bed at exactly 7:00 a.m. tomorrow.

And he hadn't even signed it.

3

PEREMPTORY AND RUDE, that was Mr. Jack Carlisle. Freddi would deal with him in the morning. For the moment, she needed to lie down and sleep. As she snuggled under the duvet, a little voice reminded her of a few other, more earthy and seductive aspects of the man who was her new employer. Those naughty whispers she would ignore. She would forget the extraordinary way her body had started to sizzle and tingle at his nearness, and how she had virtually attacked him.

How to explain her reaction to him? Simon, her ex-fiancé, had never had such an effect on her. Neither had Navy Roger, who had been The First. She should have known that, being a sailor, he'd soon move on to wilder waters.

It would be best to banish the incident from her mind and concentrate on the task at hand. Judging by the way Jack had behaved last night, she was going to have plenty to work on if she was going to transform this somewhat rough-edged fellow into a suave and polite gentleman.

BACK IN THE WIDE, king-size bed, Jack had been having a wonderful dream. But now, suddenly, his fantasy had evaporated. He squeezed his eyes shut, trying to recapture the fabulous feeling of feminine flesh snug-

gling into him. He was on the verge of success when
the telephone rang, waking him up. He groaned,
wiped his hands over his face and stretched to reach
the demanding instrument. Just as he was within
grasping distance it stopped ringing.

The sound of a woman's voice wafted through the
thin wall. Jack's eyebrows shot up. What the hell? Last
thing he remembered... Oh yeah. That voice, those cul-
tured vowels, those crisp consonants, belonged to
Freddi Elliott, the female butler from jolly old England.
Jack narrowed his eyes. Surely that luscious, fantastic,
sexy dream he'd been having couldn't possibly have
featured *her?* Nah. Impossible. The dating desert he'd
been in for too long because of all the extra hours he'd
put in at the office and the laboratory was causing hal-
lucinations.

"Hang on a sec," he heard her say. A pause. "Polly,
do you realize it's the middle of the night here?" Another pause, then, "Is Tabitha there?"

Jack pursed his lips, thinking. Well, of course she
would know Tabitha, but he would have expected Elliott to call her Mrs. James. Now the question was, did
Freddi Elliott by any unlucky chance happen to know
his archrival Simon as well? His dastardly cousin was
quite capable of planting a spy in the opposite camp.
He'd had it in for Jack ever since his family's first visit
to England.

The memory of that stay, soon after his mother died,
when he was ten and Louise was eight, rose up in
Jack's mind. That had been the start of the bad feeling
and rivalry between the cousins. Simon, two years
older than Jack and at the time a foot taller, had
mocked him from the start.

"London, *Ontario?*" Simon grabbed hold of Jack's arm and twisted it behind his back. "What kind of a stupid town is that?" he taunted. "Couldn't they even think of an original name?" That was how it began. And then, Jack beat Simon at chess, a game Simon always won effortlessly. Subsequent visits only seemed to reinforce Simon's jealousy. Every time Jack had a success, Simon had to go one better. When Jack made the hockey team, Simon got his rowing blue. When Jack completed his engineering degree in metallurgy, Simon went for an MBA.

The thing was, he didn't want Simon horning in on his project. The new method of bonding metals held tremendous promise, but Uncle Avery had said it was outside of the scope of Quaxel Corporation and had advised Jack to set up a separate company.

And the thought that Uncle Avery was being fed reports on how Jack was shaping up made him furious. Lord, the demon stress was making him paranoid. He lay on his back and squeezed his eyes shut. Maybe he'd drift right back into the dream and take up where it had left off.

SUMMONED OUT OF SLEEP by the telephone, Freddi opened her eyes to complete darkness. Disoriented, she stretched out a hand for her bedside light. Instead of a silk-covered lampshade and alabaster base, she touched cool metal. The phone kept ringing.

She found the switch and snatched up the receiver.

"Hello, Freddi," Polly's bright tones rang in her ears. "How was the trip?"

"Mmmph." Freddi dragged herself upright and

looked at her watch. "Polly, do you realize it's the middle of the night here?"

"Nah. I just got into the office. Must be at least ten-thirty."

"Is Tabby there?"

"Yeah. Hang on, she wants a word too."

"Tabby! He's expecting me to bring him breakfast in bed."

"So?"

How to explain without revealing the faux pas she'd already committed? "So, judging from—er—the sweatpants he was wearing last night I would say he's probably—er—rather virile."

"And?"

"What if I fumble when I put the tray down or something?"

"Just keep it professional and you'll do fine."

"Yeah, but I wish—"

On the other side of the drywall partition, Jack pricked up his ears. Nice to know she thought him virile...but he never discovered what she wished. Instead, her next question puzzled him.

"Any sign of that snake?"

A pause.

"Good. Remember, you promised not to tell him where I am. He's not getting it through his head that we're over. I don't need him bothering me here, too." Another pause. Freddi was relieved to hear Tabitha say, "No problem, Freddi."

"Give me a call in a week if you need me to put in a progress report. Now, I'd better be getting up and dressed if I'm going to provide His Studliness with breakfast at seven.'' After she put the phone down, she realized Tabitha never did say why she had called in the first place.

Jack leaned back against the mahogany headboard, folded his arms over his chest and gave a satisfied smirk. He wouldn't allow his suspicions to spoil his anticipation. If Freddi was here to spy on him that would be short-lived. It had been a while since he'd looked forward to breakfast with such relish. Usually he didn't bother with more than a cup of coffee. But today...today all he could think was, Roll on seven o'clock.

WIDE AWAKE, FREDDI sat on the edge of the bed. Five-forty. Time to start getting organized. First, she'd retrieve her luggage. Providing, of course, it wasn't still circling around Toronto, sight-seeing from the back of the taxi.

Clad in her overcoat, she found the light switch at the top of the stairwell. Slowly she made her way down the spiraling steps to the ground floor, wondering what lay in store for her and where her bags were. In the gloom, her toe made sudden unexpected contact with her suitcase. She almost took a tumble, but saved herself by flopping over at the waist like a puppet. How very thoughtful of Jack to leave the three packages just past the foot of the stairs. Had he intended them to act as a booby trap?

She noticed her hat, picked it up and looked for a place to put it. Ah, the marble blind-eyed bust in the entrance hall would do. In fact, she rather liked the whimsical look she'd produced.

Grabbing the handle of her suitcase, she lifted it an

inch off the floor. No way could she get this up to the
room. She'd only managed with it this far thanks to all
the kind taxi drivers. She'd really packed too much!
Thinking creatively, she decided to unpack downstairs
and carry her things up to her room.

Stealthily, she made several ascents and descents. At
last she carried up a final armful and set about preparing her uniform. A crumpled effect would not do. With
the help of the small traveling steamer she'd bought,
she got rid of the creases.

Freshly showered and dressed, Freddi checked her
appearance in front of the mirrored closet. If she was
going to be a butler she might as well look right. And if
this job could help her rebuild her life, it would make
the hassle worthwhile. It was bad enough that Simon
had totaled her car and been unfaithful to her. But the
fact that he'd run up a debt on her Visa was the big
problem. She needed to earn well to wipe the slate
clean and start over.

Her black tie was not quite properly aligned with the
collar of her white shirt, so she leaned in close to adjust
it. She tugged the points of her gray weskit over the
calf-length, pin-striped skirt, then did up the buttons of
the black dinner jacket, making sure the stiff cuffs
showed just the right amount of white below the
sleeves. Black tights were pulled up well enough so
that they didn't wrinkle, and sensible, flat-heeled lace-
up shoes shone with polish. Her hair was slicked
down, close to her skull. She then confronted her image full on. She would do. It was a pity that she had no
white rose to place in her buttonhole, but she would
soon remedy that lack.

Downstairs, she explored the living spaces. The

morning was still early, but light reflected off the snow, which meant that the house was not at all dark. In the fireplace, the ashes lay cold and gray. She looked in the direction of the black leather couch. If she ignored a certain late-night excursion, the last coherent memory she had from yesterday was of sitting there and falling asleep. On the coffee table, between the empty pizza box, a glass and a coffee mug, was a man's wallet, presumably Mr. Carlisle's. Hardly making a sound, she straightened the place up.

Into the not-too-small galley kitchen she stepped. Everything was state-of-the-art, sleek and modern. Freddi's gaze swept appreciatively over smart wooden cupboards and shiny granite tops. Underneath was the antidrudgery angel's gift to humankind, the dishwasher, and she put the soiled crockery and glassware inside. Against one wall stood the largest fridge she'd ever seen. Opposite waited an equally impressive stove that could have coped with the catering demands of a small restaurant. Mr. Carlisle must be totally into his cooking, probably a real foodie.

What a contrast this was from the hodgepodge of cupboards and appliances and single overhead light she'd left behind in Hampstead. She sighed.

The moment she'd discovered Simon shagging Polly's friend she'd taken off, gone to Paris for the weekend. He'd acted incredulous and hurt when she told him this was the end. He'd sworn he wouldn't stray again. Before making her final escape she'd retrieved nearly all her belongings, and then given her last few pounds to the airways to cover the overweight charge. That had surely been worth it. As long as Jack never found out she'd been associated with his cousin she'd be fine. She couldn't bear the thought of him knowing how she'd allowed herself to be taken in by Simon.

All things considered, this wasn't such a bad exchange. Jack's taste in clothing could do with some refining, but she couldn't fault his living style. Tabby had told her he had a trust fund from his father. Pity there was no such fortune in the impoverished Elliott family. Every penny earned went to hang on to the manor house and home farm—all that was left of a once sizable estate. Although their parents had scrimped to send both Freddi and Matthew to exclusive boarding schools, they just had to manage on their own now.

She sighed and got busy with the task at hand—preparing a good hearty breakfast.

From the stack of crockery in a glass-fronted cabinet she chose a suitable plate. Thinking to warm it, she pulled open the oven door and paused, considering the pristine interior. The shelves were still encased in plastic. Corrugated cardboard covered the elements. Revise the first conclusion. So far in its existence, Jack Carlisle's oven was all flashy surface. That could possibly apply to the man as well. Time would tell soon enough.

She turned toward the fridge and opened it to take out the necessary ingredients. The interior of the appliance gleamed empty and was almost as unused as the oven. Freddi bit her lip. Slowly she shut the door again. One after the other, she began opening cupboards. Maybe she'd find a tin of fruit and a box of cereal in the pantry. No such luck. Even the bread bin contained only a sprinkling of bread crumbs and a plastic packet.

How could she produce breakfast when there was no food available?

Arms folded, Freddi leaned back against the cabinets, looking up at the ceiling while she thought. This was a challenge. Just what she liked. Already she could feel her problem-solving energy prickling in her brain. After discarding the idea of spending valuable time looking for a store that was open this early, she gave a brisk nod. She knew just what to do. First, she picked up Jack's wallet and checked it for cash. Plenty of good-size bills in there. Fine. Back up the stairs she headed, and returned with a couple of her reference books. Then she picked up the handy kitchen phone and dialed. A smile of satisfaction spread as she replaced the receiver. That was sorted. One full breakfast was on order, as well as a continental for the staff. If this was some kind of test, Mr. Jack Carlisle was soon going to discover it was well within the bounds of Elliott's capabilities.

AT PRECISELY two and a half minutes to seven, Freddi curled her fingers around the wooden handles of the large tray. It was beautifully set and loaded with half a grapefruit, a bowl of cereal, milk and sugar, a plate of bacon and eggs, several slices of toast on the side, plus butter and marmalade and a generous carafe of coffee, all courtesy of a ritzy downtown hotel.

Outside Jack's door, she stopped. This was one of those moments when she regretted allowing Tabby to persuade her to take a crash course in buttling. But there was no need to be nervous. He needn't know she'd never done this before and didn't intend to do it again. She'd go in, put the tray down, open the curtains and remove herself. A deep breath in and out and then she knocked sharply, three times.

"Yeah, come in." His voice sounded scratchy. No reason for it to have such a strange effect on her, but it did. She'd never felt anything quite like these hitherto unknown physiological reactions she'd been experiencing since yesterday.

Stop right there, Elliott. Remember what Tabby said. This is really no big deal.

She pushed open the door. Straight away she knew she was in trouble.

4

RIGHT ACROSS THE ROOM, staring at her as if ready and waiting, Jack reclined in bed. Without the covering of the bandanna, his hair gleamed thick, wavy and black. Around him spread a sea of rumpled sheets. She wondered briefly if he'd had a rough night. But mostly, her attention was riveted on the sight of him, the impact of his presence, the dangerous way he looked this morning. Perhaps it was because of the dark shadow on his unshaven cheeks and chin, but it was mostly because of his expression. What did he do to make his eyes glitter like that? And how could he look so much like— like dynamite? His wide chest was bare, as was the rest of him, if her memory served her correctly. She dropped her gaze. Forget that, Elliott. Wipe it off the slate. Just concentrate on getting yourself and His Studliness's tray across the expanse of carpet.

"Good morning, sir." Her formal manner was well in place.

"Jack."

"Yes, sir."

He sat still, arms folded, but watching her every move. She stopped beside the bed.

Now what? She'd just known this was going to be awkward; and somehow she was sure Jack was deliberately making it difficult. Inside she may be trembling, but she wasn't going to reveal that. Ever since being sent off to boarding school at the age of eight, she'd been thoroughly educated in stiff-upper-lipness.

Her hold on the handles tightened. If she put the tray on his lap it might slide off, especially if he kept his arms folded and his ankles crossed. But there was not enough room between him and the edge of the bed to place it there. She swung away.

"I'll leave the tray on the table for you, sir."

"No, you won't."

She paused and stiffened. "I beg your pardon?"

"I said I wanted breakfast in bed, and that's what I meant."

"Yes, sir."

"Jack."

She ignored that, but carried the tray with exaggerated deliberation around to the other side of the bed. Someday she was going to discover exactly what that tattoo on his upper arm looked like.

She stepped away and went over to open the blinds. Turning back, she asked, "Will that be all for the moment?"

"Yes."

"I can draw your bath, if you wish."

"I'll take a shower, thank you."

Did he sound a little miffed? She certainly hoped so. If this was going to be a war, so be it. A battle was just what she needed to get rid of her rage against Simon. She still hadn't decided if she was more angry at him for totaling her car and then lying about it, or for being unfaithful. And why the hell had he decided to go for Polly's friend Sharon? If he had to go and shag someone else, at least he should have had the decency to choose someone Freddi didn't know.

Out in the passage, the door securely shut behind her, she put a thumb to the end of her nose and waggled her fingers. Feeling like a schoolgirl again, she grinned.

Then she sighed. How hard it was to be in a menial position. Only the promise of a fat salary and the possibility of a quick way out of her difficulties could have persuaded her to take on such a role. Thankfully, she'd been born and bred to know exactly the right way of doing things.

And then of course there was Tabby, Simon's sister, who knew all about his nasty ways and insisted that giving Freddi this job was the least she could do to make up for the trouble Simon had caused.

Freddi made a detour into her room to fetch her notebook and more reference material. In one corner of the kitchen she'd noticed a small built-in desk. For the moment she could make use of that. Tabby had suggested Jack could benefit from her office and administration skills. He'd soon find out what a mistress of organization she was. If she succeeded in being efficient, after a week he wouldn't know what hit him. Smiling to herself, she remembered the look on his face when she'd walked in with the breakfast tray. Score one for Elliott.

HAVING RECOVERED from his astonishment at his butler's achievement, Jack sat savoring the last half cup of coffee. Appreciation for the meal overcame his chagrin at being bested. Now that he was finished, he set the tray aside and got up. Once shorts and a spare T-shirt were shoved into his gym bag, he went through to his en suite bathroom to comb his hair. Reflected in the mirror stood the business whiz of the western world. Sooner rather than later, people were going to recognize his genius. If it hadn't been for the downshift in the economy, he'd be there already. As it was, instead of easily getting funding to develop the applications for his product, he'd been forced to go to Uncle Avery who had reservations about Jack because of some important negotiations he'd botched five years ago at the age of twenty-four. In spite of subsequent success, that black mark hadn't yet been erased.

Jack rolled his shoulders back. No good dwelling on such things. It was time to get the blood running. Today he was looking forward to his exercise session. Maybe he'd be able to sweat out the contradictory feelings he was having about Elliott. On one hand, he wanted her gone, out of his life. On the other, he was hooked on the vague notion that he'd been dreaming about her in gloriously vivid Technicolor. She was getting to him, invading his space, and he couldn't imagine having her around 24/7. But he was enjoying what was swiftly becoming a battle of wits.

It might be an idea to give dear cousin Tabitha a call.

He got through immediately.

"Tabby, what the hell do you mean by sending me a woman?"

"Freddi?" Her voice sounded suspiciously airy. "She's exactly what you need, Jack. Believe me, if anyone can save you, she can."

"I'm sending her back."

"No! Don't. Either Simon or you have to take over from Uncle Avery when he retires. You don't want to hand Si the job on a plate. So far, he's looking like a certainty."

"You mean, because he's Uncle Avery's godson?"

"Right. And I'm sorry to tell you, he's been spreading rumors about you again."

"Oh yeah? No doubt saying I'm uncouth and wayward."

"Er, yes.... Look. Give Freddi a chance. I'm certain you'll find she's the best thing that ever happened to you."

"Guaranteed to get me Uncle Avery's approval, is she?"

"That's what I hope. Part of it, anyhow. She'll sort you out, put you right so that you can't put a foot wrong."

There were a few seconds of silence while he absorbed that.

"Um...Jack?" Tabby's voice sounded tentative.

"Yeah."

"There's only one thing I have to insist on."

"What's that?"

"This is awkward, but I know you're an honorable man."

Nice to know someone had faith in his good qualities.

"I try to be."

"So please, what I want to ask is, don't even think of Elliott as being female."

Jack laughed, but even he could hear it sounded phony. "The way she looks, all buttoned up in that hideously severe uniform, stopping myself from hitting on her won't be any problem at all."

"I want you to give me your word on that."

He was silent while his memory nudged him back into the wisps of a dream, and reminded him of how he'd reacted when he'd carried her up to bed yesterday. "Why is this so important?"

"Partly because that's the agency's policy, and partly because...well, Freddi went through a bad time just recently." Tabitha paused, and then repeated, "So please, promise me, Jack."

"I don't think I can quite do that. Proximity, you know. All I can say is, I'll try. Anyways, I'm busy with a dating project."

"Don't say that."

"What? You don't want me to date?"

"Of course I do. We all know Uncle Avery's emphasis on the right partner in life. But it's the 'anyways' that bothers me."

"Excuse me? You want me to date both ways?"

"Stop it, Jack!" Tabby sputtered between her giggles. "'Anyway' is *singular*, not plural. So don't say 'anyways.'"

He gave an exaggerated, put-upon sigh. "Wish I could just stay plain Jack and not have to learn all this trivial stuff."

"I know it seems trivial, but decisions often hang on impressions rather than facts. And remember, my dastardly brother is scheming to be top dog, number one, the fella with all the power."

"Tabby, I just want to get on with the job. Why must I be sucked in?"

"Because you know it would be a disaster if Simon took over the reins... It's the family, Jack. You can't avoid it."

She had him there. As much as he tried, he couldn't

shake off the family feeling, partly because he felt responsible for the legacy of his father. After asking Tabitha how she and her husband were doing, Jack hung up the phone, not exactly satisfied, but at least a bit reconciled to the situation.

He went running down the staircase and paused at the bottom. Something was missing. He distinctly remembered... Freddi's luggage was gone. She'd taken the hint and removed herself, gone back to England. Great. The whole episode was a hideous illusion. Although he still wasn't too sure about that dream.

He strode into the living room to retrieve his wallet, and paused when he reached the empty coffee table. His wallet was no longer where he'd left it. Either he'd been burgled in the night or his woman butler was still at large.

Now, where was she? Scanning the surroundings, he had the idea that the whole place looked neater, which meant she must be somewhere around. He listened. Not a sound...except a rustling, like a page being turned. He headed to the kitchen to investigate.

Freddi sat with her back to him, working at that stupid desk that was too tiny for him.

Time to needle her a little bit. "Busy already?"

She half turned in the chair. "Just preparing some notes."

"Surely you've got a memory."

She sent him an admonishing look. "I don't like to take chances."

"No? Wasn't coming over here taking a chance?"

"I, er, I was more or less forced into that."

"Forced? How?" This sounded intriguing.

Her mouth pressed into a prim pout. She had no intention of going into details, crying on his shoulder, although she had to admit, Jack's shoulders were temptingly broad. "There were circumstances at home." She shut the notebook and stood up. "I'll have you know, Mr. Carlisle, it's not done to ask personal questions."

"Is that so?" Her denial increased his desire to know. He slid one hand into his back pocket, in the process pushing his pants down an inch lower. Her eyes flickered to his waist and away.

"Yes, sir."

"How'm I going to find out about you if I don't ask personal questions?" He took a couple of steps forward, crowding her. "I mean, here you are, sharing my house."

And last night, for just a little while, she'd shared his bed as well.

Freddi stood her ground. If he crowded any closer she'd be able to breathe the scent of a freshly showered Jack Carlisle.

"I'm your butler." She tilted her chin just a little more than was necessary to look him in the eye. "You don't need to know anything about me, other than that I'll work to your advantage. On the other hand," she continued, "given the scope of my job description, I'll have to find out a great deal about *you.*"

"Fine by me." He lifted his hands in a guileless gesture. "My conscience is clear. I have absolutely nothing to hide." But he wondered if *she* did.

"Good. Because I'll need to use your computer. I have to get onto the Internet and I'll need your password."

"Why?"

"All sorts of reasons. But first off, I need to order in some groceries."

Jack opened his mouth, then snapped it shut. Wariness flickered in his eyes. "What else would you do?"

"For example, download your e-mail."

He shifted from one foot to the other. "All right. I suppose that might be useful."

She looked him up and down. Didn't the man ever dress in decent clothes?

"A gentleman never goes out dressed like a—a layabout."

Legs apart, body braced, he stood in front of her. She could almost see the scarlet steam of annoyance wafting out of his ears.

"I go to the gym dressed like this," he said, enunciating every word. "Then I *change* before setting off for the office."

He'd already turned away when a thought struck him.

"Just remember, I don't want any spam."

"Sir, I would never dream of serving you anything but home cooked meals."

"Huh?"

"Spam—tinned meat."

"Oh no. I meant, junk e-mails."

She bit her lip. "I see."

Intent on getting out the door, he headed for the lobby.

Freddi stopped him. "Mr. Carlisle—"

"Jack—"

She held out the wallet. "I'm afraid I had to take out some notes to pay for the breakfast."

He took the leather folder from her and opened it up.

"Here." He held out five one-hundred-dollar bills. "Something to cover expenses. Keep two for yourself. It occurs to me you'll need some cash. Consider this a moving allowance."

She accepted the notes from him and closed her eyes on a quick prayer of gratitude. Bloody right she needed this. After the dastardly Simon's incursions, she was seriously into negative equity. As a last resort she could ask her father to help, but she'd much rather not.

Jack resigned himself. British chicks, always on the make. Well, he wasn't one to quibble about money. "Today I'll organize a debit card for you, so you can use that for the household."

Freddi shifted her weight. She dropped her gaze.

Jack noticed that her face was almost translucent. Shadows smudged the fine skin under her eyes. She looked pale, fragile.

"Feeling jet-lagged, are you?" In spite of his best efforts to stay stern, a sympathetic tone crept into his voice. "Tell you what, as you conjured up such an excellent breakfast, you can take some time off today. Catch up on that sleep you seem to need."

Dark eyes stared up at him.

"What I need is exercise," she said.

"I suppose you *could* come to the gym with me," he offered.

"No, thank you, I don't like sweat shops. And I need to get started here."

Good. That let him off the hook. "Well, please yourself, go swimming, dancing, whatever. They're all available nearby." He turned away from her.

"Thank you, sir. I think I will."

"It's Jack, dammit." Whirling around, he slapped

the wall with a flat hand. "When you call me sir you make me feel as ancient and curmudgeonly as my Uncle Avery."

"Yes, sir, er, Jack... Would you like me to answer the phone?"

"Please yourself." He stepped back. "You can write down the messages, too." Picking up his bag, he said, "In any case, I have an appointment tonight. I won't be back for dinner."

Jack was almost out the door when the marble bust caught his eye. On it, set at a rakish angle, was Freddi's hat. He dropped his gym bag, rummaged in the closet and dug out his bike helmet. Eyes glittering with malevolent glee, he removed the hat and threw it up onto the shelf. Then he replaced it with the helmet.

AT TWO O'CLOCK, Freddi went to fetch her coat. Earlier she had received the first of a weekly delivery of flowers, including roses for her buttonhole. She had just finished arranging a vase.

Now she approached the closet and did a double take. Was she hallucinating? Instead of her hat sitting jauntily on the marble bust, she saw the shiny surface and aerodynamic lines of a bicycle helmet. Huh. Obviously that belonged to Jack and he'd swapped it, not approving of her funky headwear. All right, Mr. Carlisle, she thought. This calls for retribution. Quickly, her mind ran through all the schoolgirl tricks she'd encountered or perpetrated as a boarder; tricks like short-sheeting beds and exchanging the sugar in the sugar bowl for salt. No, nothing like that would do. She'd think up something more subtle to move her pawn forward and advance her game. Meanwhile, she had a class to attend.

She set off for the dance studio and the exercise she craved. Just as Jack had said, there was one nearby. Earlier she'd consulted the directory and given the studio a call. A friendly voice had given her the particulars of available classes and told her how to get there.

Well wrapped up against the cold north wind, Freddi was curious to get more of an impression of her environment. The row of narrow town houses, obviously newly built and in keeping with the Victorian feel of other nearby properties, made her feel at home. At regular intervals along the sidewalk, bare branches of trees promised pleasant shade for the summer.

She turned up Yonge Street and passed a small supermarket. It would be good to get a few supplies on her way back. Next was a boutique that specialized in leg wear. She regarded the display. One plastic leg showed off just exactly what she needed.

Freddi was early. She might as well seize the opportunity so that there was no need to swelter any longer in Mr. Carlisle's overheated house. She'd buy three pairs of black, lace-topped, stay-up stockings. Within twelve minutes she was equipped, and riding the elevator to the dance studio.

She'd already decided to sign up for the Latin instruction, although she had given passing consideration to belly dancing. But she thought better to go with her original plan and learn to salsa.

Only, once there, she found it wasn't so easy. The Latin beat pulsed through her, her blood began to pump, but she couldn't get the hang of the dance. Even though she had studied ballet for a couple of years, her hips and knees wouldn't cooperate. How frustrating. Maybe practice would do the trick. At least she felt alive again.

WEARY FROM his long day away at the office, Jack climbed the steps. His eyes felt blurry from staring at spreadsheets on the computer, his brain was ready to shut down after straining through problem after problem. Plus, he'd endured a long and difficult evening meeting with a potential customer. He pushed his key into the lock, turned it, then paused. Inside, the lights were shining and he had the fanciful thought that they glimmered with welcome. The smell of wood smoke from a fire had him breathing in an appreciative breath.

He stepped inside, set down his briefcase and shucked off his shoes. Home sweet home. Thank goodness he'd taken the advice of his financial adviser and invested in his own house. After years of renting part of a duplex, it was great to come into peace and quiet, to know that he had the place to himself. But this was no longer true. He was about to shrug out of his leather jacket, when Freddi appeared.

5

"I'LL GET that for you, sir." She lifted the garment away from his shoulders and neck, allowing him to slide his arms out.

Jack stood still. With Elliott standing so close behind him, he'd caught a whiff of something, a subtle scent that shot him right back into the sexual fantasies that had been haunting him at odd moments all day. He barely stopped himself from grabbing her and hugging her close. Holding the newspaper in front of him, he left her to hang his coat in the closet.

Already she was changing his life, Jack thought as he wandered through to the living room. Scarlet and yellow tulips in a geometric vase graced the coffee table. A couple of current magazines were neatly layered on one side. His house felt subtly different. And he wasn't at all sure he liked that. Why couldn't things stay the way they'd been?

Unfortunately, he knew the answer to that all too well. If he wanted to be in a position to advance his cause with Uncle Avery, he had to shape up. The challenge of succeeding with his own business as well as the family company was an exciting one, and he knew he could excel. If only there weren't these stupid strings attached. If only he didn't have to bother with learning etiquette and what cutlery to use. If only his butler had been a man. He wondered what else Elliott had done today. Had she been successful in accessing his computer? For a moment he wished he could track any files she might have opened. Had she found the dummies he'd set up in case of a network security breach? Sure, he had the latest virus protection and fire wall, but he couldn't be too careful. What if she *were* a spy sent by Simon? he wondered, not for the first time. Fortunately, most of his confidential information was on his office hard drive and not at home.

"Would you like a nightcap, sir? A whiskey and soda?"

She was back to "sir," was she? And how was it that the masculine way she was dressed made her appear so softly feminine? It must be the contrast of that petite body in the strict uniform. His gaze flicked to the rose in her buttonhole, just above her breast.

He scowled at her. "No, thanks."

"Well, what about a mug of cocoa?"

Cocoa? Now, there was a cozy idea. Immediately he was back in his mother's kitchen, sitting at the pine table, his hands around the warmth of a cup while his mother listened to him as he chattered away, telling her about the day at school. He swallowed.

"Perhaps I will."

"If you'd like to sit and relax, I'll bring it to you."

Jack sank onto his favorite chair, put his head back and wiggled his toes. The fire glowed and flickered. All was quiet except for the sound of Freddi tinkering in the kitchen. He really hadn't expected her to be up, waiting for him. Before she messed with his head any further, he had to get rid of her. Already he'd worked out another impossible task. He didn't want a superior waif bossing him around, haunting his mind and interfering with his life. Within the week she had to be on a plane, heading east. Then Tabby could organize a replacement. A *male* replacement.

She came through and placed a small tray in front of him. On it sat the mug of cocoa and a plate with an assortment of cookies.

His mouth began to water. Then he noticed something missing. "Where are the marshmallows?"

"Marshmallows?"

She sounded bewildered, as if she'd never heard of them.

"Yeah. You know, pink and white mushy things—candies."

"I didn't realize you liked to eat sweets."

"Not for eating—they're for melting in the cocoa."

"Oh. I *am* sorry. We don't do that in England." She gave a sniff. "I'll be sure to get some in tomorrow."

"That'll be another Internet order, will it?"

"Yes."

"So you got into my computer." It was a statement that she didn't contradict.

There was an awkward moment while she stood still. Then she asked in a frosty tone, "Will that be all, sir?"

He was too tired to insist she call him Jack. "Yes, thank you, Elliott."

"In that case, could I ask—do you have any particular plans or instructions for tomorrow?"

Arms reaching for the ceiling, he gave a huge stretch. "Sure. I've got a date in the evening."

"And will you be entertaining at home?"

"No, I'm taking her out... Which reminds me, I need

you to do something about my car. I haven't given it a run for a while. It needs to be serviced, filled up with gas, that kind of thing."

"Certainly, sir."

Hands clasped in front of her, Freddi stood looking calm and demure. The ironic thing was, all that buttoned-up stuffiness made him want to ruffle her slicked-down hair, unbutton her jacket, her vest, her blouse... What would she look like, he wondered, in the throes of passion? With a sigh of exasperation, he registered that the wayward thoughts which had insisted on tantalizing him, on pulling him off course at odd moments of the day, were not easily harnessed. His plan to pressure her into leaving had better come off. He rose, deciding to finish his cocoa in his room. Alone.

"And would you like breakfast at seven, the same as this morning?" she asked.

Tempting, but... "No. I'll grab something at the office. I have to get an early start."

Even though Jack came downstairs before seven the next day, Elliott was prepared. The smell of freshly brewed coffee wafted from the kitchen, and the toaster waited with two slices of bread between its wiry teeth, ready to be browned. Butter and marmalade had been set out, and the morning paper signaled its readiness to be read, or at least glanced through. He couldn't resist.

Jack finished his last bite of toast, and drained the coffee mug. He got up from the table and went into the kitchen. Elliott sat working at the desk. He walked over and stood behind her, where, once again, he caught the faintest whiff of her scent. The smell went straight to his gut, re-creating his body's memory of a dream—a very sexy dream. He gave his head a short, sharp shake. Get real, Carlisle, that was nothing but an illusion. Banish the thought that underneath that strict uniform Elliott might just be soft, female and as uninhibited and passionate as his fantasy.

"Here's the key for my car." He held out the metal ring. "You know how to get into the garage, do you?"

"I discovered the door this morning, but I didn't go in."

"Fine. Then you'll have absolutely no problems."

He could barely suppress a grin of pure masculine glee. Already he could taste victory and it was sweet.

CURIOUS TO SEE what make of vehicle Jack drove, hoping, for the sake of his uncle's approval rating that it wasn't something American, Freddi made her way to the garage. She opened the door, turned on the overhead light and stepped down three steps into the cold air. There, crouching dark green and sleek, she found a sporty Jaguar. Uncle Avery, whom she knew well because of the many times she'd visited him and Aunt Tina with Tabitha on exeunts from school, would be pleased. Except, when she looked more closely, she saw the car was covered with a film of dirt. Uncle Avery would *not* be pleased.

Never mind, Elliott the Efficient would soon fix all that.

Key in hand, she went to unlock the driver's door. But the key would not slide in. She squinted at the small piece of metal. There was the wildcat logo, so it *was* a Jag key. Her fingers already feeling stiff from the cold, she tried again. No, definitely, this key didn't fit. Could it be that Jack had given her the wrong one?

Puzzled, she went to try the trunk. That worked, so she lifted the lid and looked inside. This didn't bode well at all. There was a threadbare old blanket, a couple of rusty tins, some half-squeezed tubes of goodness-knew-what, an assortment of plastic bags and yellowed newspapers. But that she could deal with later. If she couldn't get into the car itself, she wouldn't be able to start it or find the papers to tell her where it should go for servicing. She wouldn't be able to get the interior vacuumed and shined and the exterior waxed and polished, and she'd be in big trouble. Damn.

No use hanging around this icy garage. The cold was having a stultifying effect on her ingenuity. She wandered back into the house, mulling over the situation. All the signs indicated that Jack had given her the wrong key intentionally. Right this minute Mr. Smug Carlisle was probably smiling evilly and congratulating himself at having stymied Freddi Elliott.

In the kitchen she dropped onto the chair at her little desk. For a while she stared absently through the square frame of the window, at the patterned tracery of bare branches outside. Time to summon the backup troops, but who could they be? Aha.

Having discovered the CAA's number, she picked up the handset and dialed. Once she'd found out that Jack was indeed a member, she was relieved to hear a promise to help.

When the man from the CAA arrived, Freddi explained the situation. He looked surprised but unfazed. This time, she made her foray into the garage properly dressed. She wore a coat, hat and woolly gloves. For a second she wondered if she'd need a miner's headlamp attached to her forehead for a full inspection.

"Hey, hey, there you go." The man unlocked the driver's door, clearly getting into the spirit of things. "Open sesame. Tada—a—ah." His tone slid downward, like a CD losing power. "Da-damn."

Side by side, Freddi and the CAA man surveyed the shambles inside the car. There were candy wrappers, brown-stained empty coffee cartons, pens and pencils, notebooks, old floppy disks, a couple of cassette tapes with the tape unwound and spiraling crazily, two pop cans, discarded items of clothing—a faded black T-shirt and a pair of sweatpants—a single leather glove and an old cap.

Freddi gripped the steering wheel and peered inside, taking in the full extent of the mess.

"What a disaster." She straightened again. "I wonder when last Jack rode in this...if he ever did."

"Can't say, but this model is only a couple of years old."

She folded her arms and took a slow, measured tour of the low-slung sedan, shaking her head in disbelief.

She drew in a deep breath and summoned up some courage. "Let's take a look under the bonnet." He helped her put up the hood. Freddi gave a yelp when she saw the agglomeration of leaves, straw and twigs that decorated the engine.

The CAA man bent over and peered in. He shook his head. "You could almost picture a squirrel's nest in all this mess."

"Batty," she agreed.

"No, not bats, I don't think."

"I mean, this whole business is crazy." She linked

her fingers behind her back and rolled her eyes. "At least if there *were* a squirrel's nest I could have kept it as a trophy."

Maybe she could have worn it to Ascot as a hat in the summer. That might have stopped her stepmother complaining about her hair.

She slammed the hood shut. "Well, thanks very much."

"You're welcome."

They left the garage. Freddi shut the connecting door behind them. Casually, she took off her woolly hat and placed it on the smooth head of the marble bust. Couldn't have old Julie feeling cold...if it *was* Julius Caesar staring at her as blankly as usual.

"I need this all cleared up urgently and the car must be tuned. Could you perhaps recommend a garage?"

"Hmm. Might be a waste of time to go to a regular Jag dealership. You'd normally need an appointment."

"Any suggestions?"

"Yeah. I know a good independent garage. Their mechanics specialize in Volvos and Jaguars—and they'll clean it up inside and out."

Hours later she gave serious consideration to installing a hidden video camera in the garage. How she'd love to capture Mr. Carlisle's crestfallen expression when he found he'd lost the second round.

THE NEXT MORNING, after greeting his butler, Jack sat down at the table. As usual, his breakfast awaited. At one side of his place setting he saw the neatly folded newspaper. Glancing at the headlines, he decided he was just too bleary-eyed to deal with the world's problems right that minute. So he picked the paper up, unfolded the pages and checked out the cartoons. Nothing much to laugh about there.

He took a sip of grapefruit juice. The bitterness shuddered through him, shocking his taste buds. Another swallow woke him up a little more. What he really needed was coffee. He opened his mouth to yell, but there she was, at his elbow, all ready to pour a good strong shot of caffeine into his cup, the pretty-much-impossible-to-fault Miss Freddi Elliott.

"I trust everything was satisfactory with your Jag?" She lifted the glass carafe with a small flourish.

Jack gave a small nod. "Yup."

"And the new tire stood up to its initiation?"

"Without a squeal."

"The service improved the car's performance, did it?"

Cup halfway to his mouth, he stilled. He narrowed his eyes at her. She certainly was going on about this. So why was he so reluctant to hand out the praise she deserved?

"Going like a dream." Don't mention dreams, Jack. He'd had some X-rated ones again last night. "Oh yes, everything went humming along." Just like his libido.

She seemed to be satisfied with that, because she disappeared into the kitchen.

In spite of himself, he was beginning to develop a grudging admiration for Freddi. She'd conjured breakfast out of thin air, and transformed his disaster of a car into a gleaming, luxury, swanlike sedan. What he couldn't understand was why the babe from last night had left him cold. She was everything he'd told the agency he wanted, the epitome of the three s's—sexy, savvy and successful. But somehow there was no zing to their encounter, no excitement to the evening.

Freddi reappeared with two slices of buttered toast.

"Tonight I have to fly to New York for a seminar and a business meeting," he told her.

"I see."

She resisted the impulse to step away from the disturbing effect he had on her. "Do you need me to make the travel arrangements?"

"No, my secretary's taken care of that." Jack's expression changed to one she was quickly beginning to recognize. "However, I want you to check my wardrobe and pack me a bag."

Uh-oh. Freddi's antennae trembled like dillyboppers. Earlier, in the kitchen, she had decided that Jack's irritability was because last night's date probably hadn't come up to his expectations. Or maybe he didn't like losing a challenge. And now, before she'd got her breath back after yesterday's marathon of juggling, coaxing, organizing and generally running around, it sounded as if another labor of Hercules loomed before her.

6

DREAD DESCENDED on Freddi. Judging from what she'd seen of Jack's wardrobe up till now, finding good clothes for him to wear would be a challenge. To cheer herself up, she imagined him in baggy golf shorts of a bright plaid no Scotsman or woman had envisioned. But even in this aberration he still appeared...threatening.

As soon as Jack was out the door and on his way to work, Freddi went upstairs and into his bedroom. Before getting the measure of her task, she looked around. Clean lines, neutral colors and good-quality designer furniture lent the space an air of tranquillity. The only odd note was the photograph on top of the tall chest of drawers, framed in corded pewter. She crossed to have a look. A young woman stood in a garden, flowers on either side of her. On her hip she carried a small boy. They were smiling at each other, their expressions tender, loving. Jack and his mother, she was sure. Tabby hadn't told her much about Jack, but she had said that he was very involved with his work and unlikely to be around much, and that his mother had died when he was ten. That was why he'd never had all the refinements of life taught to him. And with a busy father away at work, meals had been catch-as-catch-can and seldom eaten at the table.

Freddi closed her eyes, memories of her own childhood flooding through her. She felt again her own, similar loss, although that had occurred when she was in her mid-teens, not at such a tender age. Two years ago her father had married for the second time, which was part of the reason Freddi hadn't wanted to go to him for help. The finances of the Elliott family had never really recovered from the devastating effect of heavy death duties, and with a new wife to support, she knew things were tough.

She opened her eyes with a sigh. Her mother would have encouraged her to confront the awaiting problem, and that's what she'd do.

When she looked into Jack's closet, she knew her instinct had been right. Obviously he hadn't been exaggerating when he'd said he'd been too busy over the last couple of years to attend to anything except work. The hangers clanged as she pushed one after the other to the side and flicked over his scruffy, worn jackets, threadbare denims, untidy cargo pants and crumpled shirts with torn pockets. Most of these could be candidates for donation to Sam the Scarecrow, who stalwartly defended her father's Kent fields. There was definitely nothing in here Jack could wear if he wanted to impress anyone other than a one-year-old baby or a cross-eyed, half-blind kangaroo. Now, how was she to go about fixing this?

It took her half an hour to work out a plan. After checking her reference books, she contacted the smartest men's store in town, and made an appointment with the shopping consultant. Then, from the closet she extracted a jacket and a pair of trousers so that she was in possession of Jack's vital statistics. Not the *most* vital, of course, just the measurements neces-

sary for a tailor. Lastly, she phoned for a taxi and took
off for the shopping district.

JACK WHEELED his nifty new carry-on bag into the hotel
room, set it on the luggage caddy and ran the zipper
around to open it. Inside, all was neatly packed and
stacked, just like Elliott herself. Her image jumped into
his mind, and he shook his head with admiration. *He*
might have considered the tasks he'd set her to be impossible, but they'd proved nowhere near difficult
enough for his ever-efficient butler. This meant he'd
have to find some other method of precipitating a
plane journey for her.

His own flight to New York had been uneventful
and his business-class ticket had ensured his comfort
and enough legroom. He'd purposely decided to travel
the night before his meeting and seminar so he could
be fresh the next morning, with his mind firing on all
cylinders, just like his Jag since Freddi's ministrations.
He'd better not think too much about Freddi's ministrations. It only led into the sort of fantasies he was determined to banish, so far without a smidgeon of
success.

Out of his bag he took a suit, a shirt and a contrasting
tie. Freddi had also packed a casually smart shirt that
could be worn without neckwear, which would also
work well with the suit. Then there were socks and
skivvies, as well as his toilet-article case. But the suitcase wasn't empty yet. Two cotton-knit garments were
nestled at the bottom. What the hell? He pulled them
out, holding a top in one hand and the bottoms in the
other. Pajamas! What did she think he was, some kind
of wuss or something? If he'd worn pajamas the other

night, he would never have experienced the feel of—of what? Again, the wisps of memory refused to form into a clear picture, only a vague impression was there, the impression that still puzzled and haunted him, the dream that was not quite a dream. More and more he was convinced that he'd have to put these sensations to a reality test, and sooner rather than later. How fortunate that he hadn't actually made a hands-off promise to Tabby.

MEANWHILE, back in Toronto, Freddi was on Jack's computer. If he could dislodge her hat, she could modify his screen saver. And she knew just what she was going to do—set up a banner with a message. And the message would be one that was certain to annoy His Studliness, the Prince of Imperiousness. He would read it as soon as he returned home, went into his office and booted up the computer. Then they'd see how he reacted to a little tit for tat.

With a gleeful grin, she pressed the button to start the computer. She didn't have long to wait before a simpering, blond, bikini-clad lovely appeared on the screen, her provocative pose suggesting she was about to undo the strings of her top.

"Tsk, tsk, tsk."

Freddi shook her head. This would never do. It took her a while, but eventually she found an image, a particularly severe and austere portrait of a man painted by Van Dyck. Then, using a graphic of a granny with glasses, she created the banner: Don't forget to mind your p's and q's. Remember, manners maketh the successful man.

There. Enough to needle him but not enough to really annoy.

As night fell, Freddi was about to place a cut-glass tumbler on the recently acquired silver drinks tray, when she froze. The sound of a key turning in the lock told her Jack was home. Any second now he'd open the door and she'd see him standing there.

The knowledge sent her breathing into quick, shallow mode and her heartbeat thumping up to a disco beat. She put the gleaming glass down with a clatter and a chink, taking a little less care than she intended, considering its cost. Rolling her shoulders to correct her posture, she tugged at the points of her weskit and told herself she was silly to feel so nervous. There was no real reason for Jack's presence to send her system into overdrive. Surely he couldn't be as compelling as she remembered?

Moving briskly through the dining area, she stepped down the two steps to the entrance hall. Then she retreated up one. There he was, dominating the space, large and inescapable, his dark hair curling at the ends and giving him a rakish look. When he glanced across and saw her, he got a certain gleam in his eye, and his features took on an expression of expectation. Something inside her gave a swift, sharp kick. Could it be the idea that maybe Jack was just the smallest bit pleased to see her?

"Welcome home, Mr. Carlisle," Freddi retrieved her buttling mode and went to stand behind him so she could help him off with his overcoat. Reaching up to his broad, straight shoulders, she realized she had been wrong. She had thought he might appear tamer, less dangerous in more formal clothes, but that wasn't so.

With his dark good looks, he merely appeared more formidable. *And, in the garments she'd chosen for him, even more handsome,* added the little voice in her head. She pursed her lips and told that frivolous, mischief-making alter ego of hers to shut up. She was *not* going to let herself be bowled over by Mr. Jack Uncouth Carlisle's sexiness. Still, she thought as she grabbed a suitable hanger from the closet, she certainly hadn't done herself a favor when she'd selected the charcoal, knee-length overcoat.

Just to keep herself on track, to stop herself from swooning like the heroine of a melodrama, she stepped back so she wasn't so close to him.

"I trust you had a successful trip?" She knew she should stop there, but she didn't. She changed her tone to smug and smirky. "And that the suitcase and new clothes were satisfactory?"

Jack cleared his throat, then found his voice. "Very good."

His answer was curt, but she caught the appreciation in his eyes as he looked down at her.

Just in case she'd got the wrong impression when he'd walked in, Jack scowled. "Except, you wasted my money."

"I did?"

"I can't imagine what gave you the idea I'd need pajamas."

She pressed her lips together, trying her best not to giggle.

Jack wasn't sure if that meant she was sorry, or trying not to grin. He was aware of a lifting of his spirits. For a few seconds, with Freddi standing close behind him, he'd been reeling from a double whammy. After a

meeting-crammed day, an annoying ride to Newark
and a bumpy plane trip, which had almost been can-
celed because of a spring-snowstorm warning, he'd
been feeling cranky and tired. But the moment he'd
stepped out of the cab, seen his house waiting for him,
lights shining in welcome, he'd felt better, almost re-
energized. Then, when his butler stood behind him,
right up close, he'd caught a whiff of her, that certain
alluring scent. As always it catapulted him straight
into his favorite fantasy and hit him with a two-fisted
power, right in his gut.

He heard the click of the closet door shutting, and
turned to face Freddi.

"Will you be dining in tonight, sir?" Her chocolate-
brown eyes glanced up at him, then she lowered them.

"Yes, I think I will." He regarded her carefully
schooled countenance. "Does that present a problem?"

"Not at all."

Briefcase in hand, Jack set off up the stairs, while
Freddi went toward the kitchen. Now that the master
of the house was home he would need a drink, and
later, she was planning on presenting him with a five-
course dinner. That meant she had preparations to
make. Fortunately she'd already set out the newly acquired silver tray and loaded it with crystal decanters
and an assortment of glasses. Tonight Jack would not
make use of his bar.

It wasn't long before her employer came running
down the stairs, his dark hair wet and shiny as it
waved back from his forehead. Freddi could see the
lines where he'd combed it. Jack must have taken a
shower. Now he was dressed in his loose-fitting pants
and hem-ripped-off T-shirt. She tried to keep her eyes

away from the strip of naked skin and sprinkling of dark hair around and below his navel, but it seemed her gaze had a recalcitrant will of its own.

Concentrate on the task at hand, she admonished herself, and looked up. There was no scowl on his face, which made her think he hadn't been into his computer yet. Good. She needed him to be in a cooperative mood.

"Would you help yourself to a drink, sir?" She indicated to the right.

He looked at his usually unadorned side table as if it had suddenly sprouted a few exotic ferns. "What's this?"

"A drinks tray."

He narrowed his eyes at her. She hastened to explain.

"I thought it would be a good idea for you to get used to this kind of setup. I took the liberty of buying what was necessary."

"But I've already got a perfectly good bar."

"I know, but a drinks tray will be expected when your visiting fireman arrives."

"Fireman? Did you set off the alarm? Or are you intending to set the place alight?"

No, but she wouldn't mind setting the man in residence on fire. Freddi doused the errant thought.

"Not at all. I meant, when your uncle comes. Must I explain everything to you?"

"Oh." His gaze raked her. "Maybe."

As soon as Jack had settled into his favorite chair, whiskey in hand, his feet up on the ottoman, she came and stood before him, hands clasped together in front of her.

"Mr. Carlisle, I need to talk to you."

"Is there a problem?" He lowered the glass. She saw his eyes flicker down to her rose buttonhole and linger.

"Yes, I think there is. My brief, as I understood it from the agency, was twofold. First, there's the buttling aspect, which I trust I'm carrying out satisfactorily."

"Of course you are."

Well, that was good to hear.

"Second," she went on, "the other aspect is to coach you in the elegancies and refinements of life so that you know which knife and fork to use and so on. We haven't done much of that. So far, we've had no time. You've been too busy."

Looking at her, he took a long sip from his glass, swallowed and licked his lips, leaving them shiny from the liquor.

"Isn't that too too sad." One eyebrow quirked. "Just shows you. Life doesn't always go the way Elliott orders it to."

She dragged her eyes away from his mouth. "The trouble is, the matter's getting urgent." She pressed her hands together to stop herself from wringing them.

Jack thought the fact that he wanted to make a move on Freddi was definitely becoming urgent. "Why do you say that?"

"Simply because of the phone call."

He gave his head a short, sharp shake. "What phone call?"

"I left the message on your desk."

"Didn't look at it."

Her neatly folded hands twisted. Clearly, whatever

information she was about to impart would not fill him with delight.

"Mr. Carlisle phoned from England earlier today."

"Uncle Avery?" He paused, his glass halfway up to his mouth. "What did the old f—stickler have to say?"

Another twist of her fingers. "That he's coming two weeks earlier than he originally intended."

7

"*WHAT?*"

Now her hands were still. "That he's coming two weeks earlier than he originally intended," she repeated.

"I heard what you said." He dropped his gaze. For a moment he stared into the transparent liquid in his glass. Tipping it back, he took a good swallow.

Her voice came again, quiet but determined. "I thought we could begin this evening."

Jack set the glass down on the coffee table with a thunk, thinking how this evening might develop if they *did* begin things tonight.

Freddi blinked at the noise. That glass certainly believed in living dangerously. She was starting to sympathize.

"How?" Jack asked.

She looked blankly at him. "How?"

"Yes. *How* shall we begin?"

She repressed the shiver that tried to slink up on her. "My suggestion is that I serve you a formal dinner." She indicated the table behind her. "In anticipation, I've set the table."

He nodded, considering. "I suppose that's a useful procedure to practice. Might as well take advantage of our time now."

The naughty voice in Freddi's head suggested all sorts of interesting ways they might do just that.

"We can do it tonight—"

Freddi, already on her way to the kitchen, grabbed on to the back of a chair. She only just managed to stop herself from tripping. Hot, red blood pounded through her body. She concentrated on regaining her upright posture as, with a certain amount of relief mixed in with a soupçon of disappointment, she heard Jack complete his sentence.

"—but on one condition."

"And that is?"

Jack's eyes flickered.

"I'm tired. I've had a long and stressful day. To see you wandering around dressed like that is making me depressed. I want you to wear something more attractive, more feminine."

"You want me to wear mufti?"

"Not if that's some kind of dog."

She looked down at herself, then lifted her chin. "Sorry, sir, but these are the rules. Fortunately, or unfortunately, a butler *always* wears a uniform. Appearances are important, you know."

It drove him mad when she put on that haughty attitude.

"Just a couple of small changes would improve my mood."

"Sir—" she flopped one hand just below her neck, the fingers spread out "—I'm so relieved to hear you don't want me waltzing around in a bunny tail and fishnet stockings."

The very thought made his nostrils flare and caused a tightening in the area of his body that refused to listen to his instructions to play dead. He pursed his lips. "Just remember, Elliott, I'm your employer, the one who's paying a pretty hefty fee for your services. Then there's the matter of the optional bonus."

"Optional bonus?"

"Sure. Didn't the agency tell you? You'll get extra if I'm satisfied that you've done a good job."

"That doesn't mean you can dictate how I dress."

"Doesn't it?" One black eyebrow rose.

Freddi half turned away from him and pretended to be busy rearranging the cut-crystal decanters. Should she or shouldn't she? If she went along with his request, would that compromise her position?

Jack went on. "I rather think it gives me some say in the matter." He crossed one ankle insolently over the other. "I'm a reasonable man, so how about a couple of small adjustments? I mean, if I spend the whole evening all grumpy and depressed, the next few hours are not going to be very pleasant for you."

A moment longer to line up the glasses. She was aware that, if she was to succeed in her task and win the promised bonus, she had to have his complete co-operation. She looked over her shoulder, regarding him warily. "What would you consider to be a 'couple of small adjustments'?"

Slowly and deliberately he looked her up and down. "How about, say, a change of footwear? I keep thinking you're going to stamp on my bare and tender toes with those boot-camp lace-ups you wear."

Putting her shoulders back, she turned to face him. "Maybe I can manage that."

"I presume you have a pair of shoes with high, narrow heels."

"Yes. Actually, I have." The admission came reluctantly.

She stood there, still battling with herself. Somehow she had the feeling that going along with his request would change things. But what could it hurt? He was right when he said it would be unpleasant if he remained grumpy all evening.

"Would that be all?" Freddi asked.

"No. I want you to lose the skirt."

Her eyes flared. "I beg your pardon."

"That one could carry off the frumpy prize of the decade. Wear the one you arrived in."

For a second Jack thought she was going to deny him. He saw her throat move and her nose lift a fraction closer to the ceiling. She opened her mouth and closed it. At last she said, "All right... As long as you'll allow me to teach you. You've got a lot to learn."

He gave a slow grin. "Of course. That's the deal, isn't it?"

She nodded.

"Okay then. Off you go... Now," he said.

For three seconds she stood still. Then, feet dragging, she moved toward the staircase. Jack watched her lever her way up the steps. Not longer than seven minutes later, he saw one feminine foot, encased in a sexy pump, point carefully and daintily down. It was followed by the second. He enjoyed the view of slender ankles, black-stockinged calves, knees, thighs—right up to the hem of the black miniskirt. Boy, was he glad he was a man who could appreciate a shapely set of legs on a woman. His French-maid fantasy nudged at his mind. He imagined Freddi coming toward him, settling herself on his lap and twining her arms around his neck. Damn. It was crazy how she could get him going.

As Freddi reached the bottom of the stairs and began to sway toward him, he grinned in satisfaction. What a kick, to turn his prim-and-proper butler into a sex kitten. Lolling back, elbows out, his hands cupped the back of his head.

"That's better. Those heels will have me feeling much more cheerful. Make sure you wear them tomorrow, too."

She came to a stop in front of him.

"Jack," she protested, "I can't possibly wear these all day. I'll be crippled for life."

He waved a hand at her, delighted that she'd forgotten to address him formally. "Okay, okay. When I'm here in the evening—that will do. All things considered, maybe it's just as well. The total effect is rather tantalizing—reminds me of Liza Minnelli in *Cabaret*. Except your eyes are not as big as hers."

Freddi caught the teasing note in his voice and fluttered her eyelashes at him in what she hoped was an insolent manner.

"And," he went on, "I'm not sure about the hairstyle."

That was too much. "There's nothing wrong with my hair!" She couldn't keep the exasperation out of her voice. "I'll have you know I had it cut in Paris."

"I see. The street-urchin look, no doubt?"

"No! Gamine!"

He grinned at her, a devilish, triumphant smile that revealed his even, white teeth. He was obviously pleased that he'd provoked her into showing some passion.

Freddi pressed her lips together and retreated to the kitchen. Any minute now, when her boss sat down to eat, she'd get her revenge. She would turn his own ex-quisitely set table on him, and he'd be in *her* power rather than the other way around.

It wasn't long before she had everything ready. Emerging from the kitchen, she found Jack lounging back, eyes closed, his whiskey glass empty. She hated to disturb him.

"Would you like another, sir?"

He started, opened his eyes and gave her a slumber-ous look. "No, thank you, Elliott."

How was it that everything he did made him more attractive to her? She'd love to go over and stroke his hair, ruffle his feathers. Sigh.

"In that case—" she drew in a breath "—if you're ready, dinner is served."

He unfolded himself from the chair and stood up. Freddi suppressed a tiny shiver. Jack was too close and so big. She wasn't accustomed to such overwhelming maleness. Yet, she felt drawn to him, just like Eve to the forbidden fruit, wanting to reach out and touch, and maybe even...bite. She couldn't help wondering how it would feel if he actually bent down and took her into his arms.

In a gigantic stretch, knuckles up, he reached for the ceiling.

"Ahem..."

Arms now reaching toward the walls, Jack stilled.

"Something wrong?"

"I'm afraid so." She stepped away from him. "I have to point out that stretching in public is not polite."

He lowered his arms. "I'll bear that in mind."

What a relief. He'd taken that docilely enough.

Freddi moved to stand behind the dining-room chair, pulling it out and holding on to the top. As Jack sat down, she pushed.

He lowered his head and stared at the sparkling array of cutlery and glassware. Unable to stop herself, she observed his reaction.

"What the hell? Where did all this stuff come from?"

"Ashley's, sir. I found them to be most obliging. I put it all on your credit card. You said I could get anything we needed."

"True." One large, spread hand hovered over the lined-up silverware. "But do I actually need—er—two spoons, four different forks and three knives?"

"Indeed you do," she said earnestly, "if you're to become thoroughly acquainted with the proper etiquette of a formal dinner."

"All this?" He waved a hand over the place setting Freddi had painstakingly and meticulously composed. "It looks like I'm about to undertake some kind of training for a battle—a duel, maybe." He picked up a knife and pointed it forward. "What'll it be, knives, forks, spoons or stemware?"

Freddi cleared her throat. "You should never pick up or hold a knife like that."

Jack put the knife down with a melancholy and exaggerated sigh. "Why can't I have one knife, one spoon and one fork like I get at any reasonable restaurant?"

"Because this is the kind of place setting you'll find at a formal dinner—official, or unofficial."

"Ah, well, bring on the dancing girls. I'll need something to entertain me while I sit chewing through all this."

Her gaze met his.

"No dancing girls," Freddi said breathlessly, and thought about salsa class. "Just consommé to start."

"If there're no dancing girls, how'm I going to consummate what?"

"Ja-ack," her tone held a note of warning. He seemed to be suppressing a smile. "You're going to eat some clear soup."

He looked up and back at her. "With what?"

"With the soupspoon."

If she was going to be so bossy, ordering him around like this, it was only fair that he should extract some fun out of the situation.

"Which one is that?"

"The one on the right."

His hand touched the spoon and fork that bridged the two sides of the place setting. "This one?"

"No. Those are for the dessert."

"Show me, then."

He leaned back. She obliged him by doing just what he was angling for—she leaned forward. How sweet. A lock of her hair whispered past his cheek, soft breasts pressed into his left shoulder. Jack closed his eyes, took a long breath in to capture her scent, and went with the flow.

"Cool," he murmured.

"What was that, sir?" The voice in his ear was soft, and husky.

"I—er—was commenting on the feel of the—ahem—silver."

"Oh." Her breath caressed his cheek. "You want the one with the round bowl."

"Are you sure about that?"

"Quite sure."

Deliberately, he put his hand on the small knife.

"No, that's the butter knife."

He put his left hand on a fork.

"No, that's the fish fork, Jack." Her voice was no longer so close and betrayed a certain amount of amusement. "Please, take your napkin and spread it on your lap. That's the first thing to do."

"I thought you said consummate was the first thing."

"No!"

That was a quick response—too quick. Did it perhaps indicate that his proper butler had sex on her mind, just as he had?

"Okay." He tried to sound meek and gave serious consideration to the idea of asking her to put the napkin on his lap for him. Maybe that would be stretching it. But why not give it the old college try?

He pushed his chair a little away from the table.

"Where are you going?" she asked.

"Nowhere."

She cocked her head in inquiry.

"Just giving you some room."

"For what?"

"So you can spread my napkin for me."

Her eyes grew round. He saw her swallow, and chew her lip.

"In a private home," she said, "you have to do it yourself."

"Chicken," he muttered.

"Not at all. It's *beef* consommé, sir."

She could play innocent all she liked, but he wasn't fooled. In fact, all things considered, he was feeling rather encouraged. Perhaps he could push her just a little more.

He made conjuring motions over the place setting. "Please show me exactly which of these bloody implements to use. Then I'll begin."

She put her hand on his. Both of them froze. He heard a little gasp. Then she lifted his hand and guided it to the correct spoon.

"This is for the soup...but," she explained, "if you're eating with old silver, which you could well do, you'll probably find a large, serving-size spoon instead."

Jack blew out a breath and prepared to tuck in. The correct spoon was halfway to his mouth when Freddi appeared with a bottle wrapped in a white cloth.

"A little sherry, sir."

"Sherry?" he asked, an incredulous note in his voice. "That's a drink for old ladies."

"One customarily serves sherry with soup, and incidentally—" her voice took on a chiding tone "—it's my second favorite tipple."

"Uh-oh. I'm sorry, Elliott."

"Apology accepted."

The bottle made a voluptuous glug-glug sound as she poured it into the smallest of the glasses grouped on his right.

"But you should try to watch what you say." She continued, "You don't want to give offense—unintentionally, that is."

"Ouch." He sighed and picked up the small glass. Holding his pinkie out in what he hoped was a delicate manner, he took a sip.

"And may I inquire," he went on with exaggerated

politeness as the fortified wine warmed his throat, "what is your first favorite?"

"Noilly Prat vermouth, sir."

Was it his imagination, or had she lingered near him longer than was necessary? This playing dumb was a good strategy. He'd employ it to the full, draw out the proceedings and see how close he could get to putting his little sexual experiment into place. In New York, he'd decided he'd have to find out, once and for all, if what his body remembered was reality or merely a very vivid fantasy.

Maybe tonight could be the night.

8

FREDDI BROUGHT IN the next course.

She placed an oval plate in front of him. On it lay a crispy, golden fish, a quarter of a lemon and a garnish of curly parsley. As she took her hand away, her arm brushed his.

"I had a hard time finding nonfilleted fresh sole, but here it is—sole meunière," she said.

These fleeting touches of hers were giving him a hard time. He adjusted the napkin on his lap.

"Now, remember, the trick with cutlery is to work your way from the outside in."

She hovered just out of range, making him itch to grab hold of her and pull her down, onto his lap. Then he'd show her just how skillful he was at working his way from the outside in.

"So, as you can see, next are the fish eaters."

He picked up the knife and fork. "These are, er, sharks?"

"Sharks? How can they be?"

"You said they were fish eaters."

"Because that's what they're called."

"Oh."

She kept an eye on Jack to see how he'd tackle the sole. Before he put himself in danger of death by swallowing a fish bone, she intervened.

"No, no. Let me show you." She moved to his side

again and pointed. "First, you cut off these little bones down the side. Then you scrape the flesh from the spine. You'll find it'll come away quite easily. Once you've eaten that, you turn the whole thing over and do the same again."

Rolling Freddi over sounded like a good idea to Jack. He even managed to carry out her instructions without any difficulty.

Freddi continued to hover and watch him carefully. Whenever she thought there was some little slip or inadequacy, she gave pointers. He had no problem with the glasses, but really, she couldn't imagine why he was making such a big deal about which knife and fork to use. Time and again he got a confused look on his face and she was forced to lean over to help him.

After the main dish of beef, Elliott removed the salt and pepper. Jack clutched on to the large wineglass, still containing an inch of dark red burgundy, as it if were his lifeblood.

She sent him a smile of encouragement.

"Don't worry, I'm not going to wrest that from your grasp. It's perfectly permissible to finish off your wine with the cheese. Later, of course, if you were, say, spending the weekend at a stately home, the women would get up from the table after the sweet course and leave the men to their port."

"Help me out here. I never remember which side is port and which is starboard."

"No, no. That's to do with sailing. I mean port—a fortified wine. What's important is to know which way around the table you have to pass the bottle. And my advice to you would be *not* to drink too much."

"Even if I'm an amusing drunk?"

She shrugged. "No. Although it's acceptable to get slightly tiddly."

"Tiddly? I thought that was some kind of kiddie's game."

Freddi gurgled. "Tiddlywinks—quite different."

Jack winked at her.

How could a simple little spasm of the eyelid cause such devastation to her system?

She hovered near his left shoulder. "A little more wine?"

He waved a hand at her. "Sit down, Freddi, for God's sake. Have a glass with me."

"No thank you, sir." She kept the bottle clasped against her breastbone as if it was shielding her from some unspeakable fate.

"Why not?" Suddenly his hand shot out and clasped her wrist, drawing her forward so that her thighs pressed against his. Releasing his hold, his arm curved around her waist.

"That would be—" she gasped for breath "—inappropriate."

Hmm. This was promising.

The phone rang. She moved away.

Damn.

"Pay no heed," Jack said, casting his napkin next to the place setting. "I'll get it."

Freddi grasped the top of the chair and closed her eyes. She blew out a breath. He'd get it, all right, if he carried on like this. He had it, no question. She'd been about to agree to have a glass of wine with him, and that would have spelled disaster. She had denied him, true; but her greater concern had more to do with the effects of alcohol than propriety. She knew what two or three glasses of wine did to her. They had the ability to affect her brain and the position of her limbs. She was sure it wasn't only Simon's boyish charm that had caused her to fall for him, that champagne had been a contributing factor in her succumbing. And once he'd got his oar in, she'd felt committed to him. Only later did she discover that commitment was entirely one-sided.

Meanwhile, it might be prudent to retreat to the kitchen.

Once he'd finished with the call, Jack again sat in solitary splendor, all too aware that the mood had been broken. He scowled at the piece of Stilton. Even the cheese she served had to have blue veins and be British. Why couldn't she go for something local like Monterey Jack?

Jack finished his wine. Soon Freddi reappeared with a small cup and saucer.

"What's this thimble you've set in front of me?"

"It's a demitasse of black coffee. And if you like, I'll bring you a liqueur... Cointreau or Grand Marnier."

"No Kahlúa?"

She shook her head.

"In that case, no, thanks."

He caught her look of chagrin.

"We'll keep the liqueur bit for another time," he said.

Unfortunately, he'd have to keep the Big Move for another time too. With her back to him, she opened a drawer, leaned forward and began stowing away the silver knives, forks and spoons.

She turned and caught Jack's gaze on the length of leg revealed by her miniskirt.

"Yo dude," she said.

Jack blinked. Freddi never used slang. "Excuse me?"

She gave her head a little shake. "That's what you said when you answered the phone. It's not the way to greet anyone."

"No? Tell me, what would you suggest? In North America, 'hi' is acceptable for a casual situation."

"Maybe. But even 'hello' can still sound rude to the British."

"What then?" he asked, his hand on the dimmer switch.

"Say 'good morning' or 'good afternoon' or 'good evening.'"

"That's too much to keep in my head just now. It's too full of all that other stuff, and my mind's on shutdown." Jack turned the knob until it clicked. The lights went off, leaving them in the dark. "So let's just say 'good night.'"

THAT WEEKEND, Jack had three date nights in a row: Friday, Saturday and Sunday.

On each occasion, he had the cheek to ask his women to come to the house so that they met there. This meant Elliott was the one who opened the door to them.

Friday night's female was tall, blond and stacked. Unfortunately, for Jack her personality was small, dull and flat.

She wrinkled her nose at Freddi. "Have I got the right address? Does Jack Carlisle live here?"

"Oh yes, madam." Freddi adopted her most formal, her most snooty tone of voice. "He's expecting you. Do come in."

Miss Friday took a small step inside. "Like, who are you?"

"I am Elliott, madam. Mr. Carlisle's butler."

The babe blinked at Freddi as if she thought she was an apparition from a Dracula movie. "Are you English or something?"

"Or something," Freddi murmured, turning away to open the coat closet. Miss Friday drifted into the hall and stood there, a vague look in her improbably turquoise eyes.

Freddi went behind her, to help with her coat. When the babe didn't move, Freddi put one hand on her shoulder. The woman leaped away and whirled around. Eyes wide, she stared at Freddi as if she thought she was about to be molested.

"Your coat, madam." Freddi waved the hanger she held in her other hand. She felt like using it as a cattle prod.

"Oh. Yeah. Sure."

Once the garment was safely behind doors, Freddi ushered Miss Friday into the living room where earlier she'd set out snacks and drinks. Then Freddi wound her way upstairs and knocked on Jack's bedroom door. What, she wondered, was he doing in there? Maybe he stood in front of the bathroom mirror, freshly showered, a towel knotted around his waist.

Freddi grinned. She'd never realized she could entertain such thoughts. But maybe it was just Jack Carlisle who brought out that part of her nature. If anyone could do it, he could... Ah, if only she could be his date, have a legitimate chance with him. But she wasn't blond, and she was his butler. She'd known it was going to be difficult, being in that position, but she'd never dreamed the reason would be because she was attracted to her employer.

The object of her fantasies opened the bedroom door. Freshly shaven and dressed in a midnight-blue, open-necked shirt, he looked and smelled wonderful.

"What is it, Freddi?"

She blinked at him. What was it she had on her mind, apart from him? Oh yes.

"Your date awaits, sir."

Downstairs again, she hovered in the kitchen for a while in case Jack required her services. She polished a glass here, straightened a few jars there, and wiped the already pristine countertops. Straining her ears, she heard the deep rumble of Jack's voice, and then the reply.

"I...like, um, agree."

Clearly, this candidate was heavy going on the conversational level. Although, maybe that wouldn't bother Jack. He was all too obviously after some other virtue. However, this woman would make a less-than-stellar impression on Uncle Avery.

Silence. Suddenly a large, dark shape shadowed the doorway—Jack, with a wild, desperate look in his eye.

"We're leaving now."

"Very good, sir."

"I'm taking her to a movie."

"I understand."

More than he realized, probably.

"Any suggestions as to what we should go see?"

Freddi smirked at him. "There is that new horror movie."

Jack's face lit up. "Great idea. Then she'll have plenty of motivation to cling to me."

Freddi sent him a daggered look. "If that's your wish, it would probably do the trick, sir."

Jack turned on his heel, and, with a jaunty step, went to rejoin his date. Freddi decided to leave them to it, and that she was just angry enough not to wait up for her employer to come home. She'd had enough of His Studliness for one night.

In an effort to distract herself from imagining Jack and his date cozying up to one another in the movie house, Freddi went to her room and picked up the romantic suspense novel she'd bought on her way back from salsa class. If that didn't keep her mind from straying to what Jack was up to with Miss Friday, nothing would.

A couple of hours went by. Her eyelids began to droop. The book fell out of her hands. Sitting up, she glanced at her bedside clock. Almost midnight, and she was still in her uniform and feeling hot. Why hadn't she taken it off before getting so immersed in that story?

She got up and began to undress. What a blissful relief to shed all those clothes and get naked. From under her pillow she slid the short, slinky, spaghetti-strapped nightie that Tabby had given her as a parting good-luck present. The silk shimmied down, lightly touching her body, whisper thin and cool against her skin. Now she'd just hop across to the bathroom and brush her teeth.

The door groaned a little as she opened it, but otherwise the house was quiet and dark. No need to bother with her fuzzy bathrobe, which would make her too hot. The coast was clear. Jack was still out on his date.

In the bathroom, Freddi meticulously cleaned, toned and moisturized her skin. Then she spent a full three minutes getting her pearly whites pristine. Fine. She could creep into bed and not give His Studliness another thought.

A quick check as she opened the bathroom door reassured her that the house was still dark. She turned back to the vanity to pick up her glass of water and stretched out a hand to switch off the light. Just before she did so, a tousled-haired Jack took the last step up into the passage. He froze.

Freddi gave a squeak, twirled across the carpeted gap and got herself into her room. As she shut the door she heard a very soft, but unmistakable wolf whistle. Footsteps stopped outside her door. She held her breath, her skin hot, her heart pounding. Slow seconds went by, and then the footsteps retreated.

She blew out a long breath and tiptoed over to the bed. As her rush of surprise and panic subsided, it was replaced by a feeling of having missed out. If she'd been bolder, had stood still instead of bolting like a scared squirrel, then maybe, right this minute, she'd be in Jack's embrace. What she should have done was to slink up to him, ask him about the movie while reaching up to straighten his collar.

Freddi let out a long sigh and snuggled down. That was just wishful thinking. She shouldn't feel disappointed. And there were a couple of consolations. Jack had very definitely been all on his own, and, unlike Miss Friday, Freddi would still be around tomorrow.

MISS SATURDAY stepped into the entrance hall with languid grace. Shrugging off the camel-colored cashmere coat that set off her sleek magenta bob to perfection, she allowed Freddi to take the garment from her. She looked around, her eyes lingering on a large, modern oil painting on the wall near the stairs. Freddi got a quick visual of Garfield with dollar signs in his eyes. She was almost beginning to feel sorry for her employer. If Jack ended up with one of these women, she could see plenty of trouble ahead.

By now she knew the routine. Jack and his date would sit chatting over a drink for a while and then they'd go out. Freddi had already made a reservation at a discreetly expensive restaurant. She was certain that would score points with Miss Saturday. Back in the kitchen, Freddi picked up a handy carving knife and tried not to think of Jack scoring. Her fingers curled around the horn handle.

She puttered about, doing her best not to listen to the muted conversation, but nevertheless aware of its awkward edge. As before, Jack appeared in the doorway.

"We're leaving now."

"Very good, sir."

"I hope it will be." He lingered for a moment, one hand on the door frame, just looking at her. She thought he was going to say something, but he just stood there. Then he dropped his hand and turned away.

LATE THAT NIGHT Freddi lay in her bed trying to get to sleep, trying not to think of Jack and his date. Eventually the rattle of the front door being unlocked announced his return. She tensed. Was he alone, or not? Quietly giving in to temptation, thinking she was growing increasingly good at that, she got out of bed, crept to the open door of her room and lurked in the shadows at the top of the stairway. Her breathing sounded loud in her ears, but no noise floated up from below. Was that a good sign or a bad one? She leaned over the railing. The downstairs light shone on Jack's dark hair. He hung up his coat, then started up the stairs.

There was no one with him.

Relief flowed through her in a warm stream. She clung onto the railing, swayed back, then forward.

Beneath her, Jack hesitated, one foot on the bottom step. He looked up. Freddi just managed to jerk back in time.

She darted into her room and shut the door. To her the click sounded as loud as a gunshot.

Just before reaching the second floor, Jack paused again, his hand on the banister. Was that Freddi's door he'd heard clicking shut? No strip of light showed underneath, but still... With last night's tantalizing glimpse still extremely fresh in his mind, he wondered if he'd just missed out on a second, similar experience.

The next morning he sat alone at the dining table eating his breakfast. Freddi hovered nearby. Or make that Elliott. Today she was very much in her butler mode and, although she pretended to be otherwise occupied, she was obviously watching him.

He started on the cereal.

"Oh, no, Jack, you mustn't do that."

"What?" Spoon halfway to his mouth, he paused.

"Hold your bowl up in front of you. You should leave it on the table."

"It's a long way between the table and my mouth," he complained.

With the arrival of the toast, he ran into trouble again. He grabbed two pieces straightaway and put them on his side plate.

She was at his elbow, about to fill his coffee cup.

"One at a time, Jack," she admonished. "No one's going to snatch the second piece away from you, and the concept of toast is not leaving the planet."

Meekly he replaced a slice, sliding it into the grid.

"Freddi," he began, "you know that woman I took out last night?"

She finished pouring and stepped back. "Yes?"

"Talk about mercenary!" he went on. "She was totally focused on the material world."

"Really?" One small hand cradled the warm carafe.

He gave a crisp nod and, both elbows on the table, waved his toast in the air.

Freddi opened her eyes wide. "Don't wave food around... And no elbows on the table until you're an uncle."

"I *am* an uncle."

"Still, I'd advise you to keep them off."

With an exaggerated sigh, he complied, then bit into his toast. The crunching sounded in his ears like firecrackers going off. He waited for Freddi to say something, but she was quiet.

Jack expected her to retreat to the kitchen as she normally did. Instead, she put the carafe down on the sideboard.

He swallowed his mouthful and said, "You should have seen the look in her eyes when she saw the Jag. Then she started pumping me about Uncle Avery. How she knew about him and the family corporation, I don't know."

For once Freddi seemed to have lost interest in coaching and buttling. She dropped into a chair, facing him across the table and leaning on her forearms.

"Maybe from the dating agency?"

"They don't give out those kind of details."

Encouraged by her attention, Jack continued, "I mean, I'm not averse to wealth. I enjoy my money." He took a sip of hot coffee.

"Don't slurp when you drink."

"But it'll burn my mouth if I don't." He wondered if Freddi's kisses would be hot. Just thinking about embracing her made him warm.

"Then you'd better wait till it's cooler."

He thought she'd get up and go away, but she continued to sit there, as if she was thinking things over.

"You work hard for it." She must have read his puzzlement, because she added, "Your money, I mean."

"Sure, but you know, it's a kind of game."

"How do you mean?" She cocked her head, obviously interested.

"Well, it's the thrill of seizing on an inspired idea, envisioning the possibilities, putting a strategy into place, making things happen." He could see she was with him, so he went on. "Business is fun, a gamble. You win, or you lose."

"And I'm here to help you win."

9

THE WORDS HUNG in the air between them. But they also seemed to remind Elliott of her duties. To Jack's disappointment, she got up and started clearing away his dishes. All too soon she vanished into the kitchen.

After a while he followed, on the pretense of wanting a third cup of coffee. Freddi was busy at the sink, so he moved in close behind, crowding her, enjoying the effect. The sweet, ivory nape of her neck was revealed to him. He was close enough to blow on it. What would she do if he pressed his lips to her skin?

Her shoulders tensed, rising a fraction. He wondered if she'd stopped breathing. When she turned her head a little toward him, Jack grinned. He rather enjoyed that his proximity unsettled her.

"I'm glad you're on my side, Fred."

She dropped a plate onto the counter with a clatter. Slowly turned to face him, her expression fiery. He wasn't sure if that was because she was uncomfortable or angry.

"No one calls me Fred," she said. "Not ever. Not even Tabby."

"Tabby?" All his nasty suspicions jumped to the front of his mind. He took a step back and narrowed his eyes. "You mean Tabitha Sherbourne—er, I mean, James?"

She gave a stiff little nod, as if she hadn't meant that to escape.

"Tell me, er—Elliott—just how well do you know Tabitha?"

"Um, we were best friends at boarding school."

"And now?"

She shrugged.

"So of course you know her brother, Simon."

Freddi looked guilty and bit her lip.

Jack was about to press on, to ask her how well she knew his rival, when the phone rang. Freddi snatched up the handset, stated the number, then handed it over. Jack decided to examine the ramifications of this revelation later. A nasty feeling churned in his gut. Just when he was beginning to appreciate his butler, to enjoy having her around, he found out that she had a more-than-casual connection to that snake, Simon.

Conversation over, Jack put the receiver down.

"Last night, when I came in, I heard a sort of scurrying." He stroked his jaw. "I'm wondering if we've perhaps got mice."

"Mice, sir?" she asked, as if she'd never heard of the small rodents.

"You know, those little grayish-brown things with whiskers—" he wiggled his fingers next to his mouth "—and cute, perky ears. All downtown-Toronto houses have them from time to time."

Haughtiness switched to horror. "You mean—" she swallowed "—we're *really* likely to have mice running around?"

Jack rather liked that "we." He grinned. So his unflappable butler was fazed by mice, was she?

"Oh yeah. Once, I got out of bed and one ran over my foot."

He flexed his bare foot, as though the little creature had just passed over it.

"Noooooo." She clutched the edge of the kitchen counter. "I hate mice. I'll get in some traps right away."

"Otherwise, if it gets bad, we can call in the exterminator."

She swallowed and nodded, looking relieved and grateful.

He chuckled.

"Tonight I've got another date. I know it's your night off."

"I can get things ready in any case."

"Any plans?"

"Me? Yes, actually. I've got an invitation. A friend of my brother's is in town. I'm meeting him at a pub—something like the Goose and Gherkin?"

"The Fox and Firkin?" Jack asked, referring to a popular spot just around the corner.

"That's it."

Jack's ever-fertile mind presented a visual of Freddi, clad in her miniskirt, sitting on a bar stool, those fabulous legs crossed, one thigh over the other. Oh man. He had to stop this. Thinking about Freddi was interfering with his enjoyment of other women, making him unable to give them a fair chance. Tonight he'd go all out to impress his date, and do everything possible to let her impress him.

"By the way, Mr. Carlisle Senior phoned while you were sleeping."

"From heaven or hell?"

"I'm sorry, I don't understand."

"My father, Mr. Carlisle Senior, has been dead for three years."

One hand flew to her cheek. "Oh sh—oot. I apologize... I meant, Mr. Avery Carlisle, from London."

Jack raised his dark eyebrows at her. "Dear old Unc. What did he have to say?"

"That I should remind you of the importance of the right spouse. He's hoping you're making progress in that area."

Jack's eyebrows descended into a dangerous scowl. "I'm doing my d—dating best."

Freddi clasped her hands in front of her waist. By now he knew this meant she had something to say.

"Okay. At the risk of your telling me public expectoration is unacceptable, Elliott, I suggest you spit it out."

She jerked her head back in a small movement that made the tip of her nose point higher. "It occurs to me, sir, that you might want to reassess your requirements."

"My requirements for a woman? Why?"

She shifted her weight from one foot to the other. His butler was wearing those cursed lace-up shoes again. Altogether, she looked laced up, from her head to her toes. One of these fine days he'd like to unlace, undo, uncover...

"Mr. Carlisle probably has different criteria from yours."

"What do you guess mine are?"

"From what I've seen so far...er..."

"In the words of Austin Powers, shagability—is that it?"

She nodded.

"What's wrong with that?" he asked, becoming irritated.

"Nothing, sir. But your uncle will be expecting a woman with *some* skill at conversation. A man is known by the company he keeps."

"And, by implication, the women he sleeps with."

It took her a moment to reply to that sally. "Never end a sentence with 'with.'"

"Hmm." He scratched his head, deciding to ignore that one. "From the details she gave me in her reply, it sounded as if the first candidate might have fitted the bill. Too bad she didn't wait around for me to answer the doorbell."

A rosy stain touched Freddi's velvety skin with a blush.

"Ah, well, water under the bridge—or, in this case, snores from the butler on the sofa."

She wished he hadn't reminded her of that night. The remembrance of being in his bed, wrapped in his arms, close to his skin, lost in his kiss, breathing him in—all that still haunted her. Lucky he didn't know how much or the reason why. Lucky he couldn't log into her mind and view the fantasies she'd been having about him, how she'd imagined him coming into her room, finding her standing on the other side of the door. He would kiss her, his hands sliding over the slippery silk until he removed that wisp of a nightie and... Whew! Jack's house really was very warm. Maybe she should ask him to turn down the thermostat.

THE ATMOSPHERE in the neighborhood bar wasn't quite the same as Freddi's favorite London pub, but it was still cheerful. Surrounded by chatter and laughter, the chink of glasses, the *sshhhrr* of the beer being pulled out of the draft barrel, Freddi prepared to relax. How glad she was to be able to shed her Elliott persona for a few liberated hours.

This evening, she'd gone as far as she could to leave her butler image behind, gelling her hair, slathering on the mascara, glossing her lips, then spritzing her wrists, behind her ears and her neck with Envy. She'd chosen to wear her clingiest, reddest top with a shade of lipstick to match. For a few, dreamy minutes she'd imagined that she was getting ready for a date with Jack, that she was his chosen companion for the evening, that he would wine and dine and romance her. But when she looked in the mirror, instead of herself, she saw Miss Saturday. No, Freddi Elliott wasn't the kind of woman Jack went for. Her hair wasn't right, her body wasn't lush enough. Even if she fancied him, that was just lust, and even if he teased her sometimes, that was just his normal behavior.

Wishful thoughts long out of her mind, Freddi was enjoying Michael's company. They'd known each other for years, and she looked on him as a second brother. He was a lawyer who'd been living in Luxembourg, working with the European government, and it had been a while since they'd spent any time together.

After pausing for a sip of beer, Freddi continued her story about Jack and the Jag.

When Michael stopped laughing, he said, "He's giving you a hard time?"

She took another swig. "He *was*, but things seem to have shifted since he got back from New York."

"Matthew told me things turned sour for you in London. How did you ever fall for that blighter, your ex?"

"He's my friend Tabby's brother. Occasionally he'd come to visit her at boarding school. I always had a crush on him because he's really handsome. But then, a couple of years later, we met properly at Tabby's wedding... Think *Four Weddings and a Funeral*. There was a band and dancing. Simon dances divinely. I was fairly high on champagne, thought I was in heaven, thought I was in love." She bit her lip. "And that was my downfall."

There was silence while they both swallowed more beer.

"At first it was good," she continued. "I was mad about him—totally infatuated. We knew the same people, so it worked well socially. And Simon hid his worst aspects from me."

"They were?"

"Oh, apart from his extravagant habits...his jealousy, his fierce competitiveness, and mostly, his infidelity." She ticked them off on her fingers. "When I accused him of being unfaithful, he was astonished that I'd expected exclusivity." She let out a long sigh. "I tend to believe what people tell me. Too trusting, I suppose."

"How long were you together?"

"Nine months. But I should have ended it long before. It was only six weeks after we got engaged that I began to realize what was going on."

"Why didn't you?"

"I suppose I couldn't let go of the idea that he was

The One for Me. It was hard to relinquish the dream, to face the truth."

"And?" Michael sat forward, forearms on his thighs, clasping his beer in two hands.

"Eventually I couldn't fool myself any longer. Tabby knew I was miserable. She knew I needed to get away, make a new start, and pressed me to take this job."

"Good for her."

Somehow, in the telling, Freddi started feeling a little better about the whole debacle.

She finished by saying, "So you see, it's important for me to make a success of this assignment. I need to feel better about myself. Not to mention the fact that I have to earn enough money to set myself back on my feet. Another thing Simon did was max out my VISA card—and he never paid a cent of it off. I just hope my talent for trouble hasn't crossed to North America."

"Well, if things should happen to turn disastrous here, or get to a point where you need legal advice, I'd be happy to help."

"Thanks. So far everything's going okay, but I'll bear that in mind."

Freddi snuggled back into her chair, thinking how heartwarming it was to be with a friend again.

TOTALLY DISGUSTED with himself and his inability to relate to his procession of lovelies, Jack slammed the door of his Jag and pressed the switch to close the garage door. The grinding noise provided an appropriate accompaniment to his aggravated mood. Another wasted date. What was wrong with him? Did he have no discrimination when it came to picking women? Where was his fairy godmother when he needed her?

Lori had sounded so perfect, her vital statistics so...vital. But then, without meeting her beforehand, without even speaking to her over the phone, how was he supposed to know she had a flapping mouth and a strident edge to her voice? Conversing via e-mail hadn't given him a clue.

He didn't mind the wasted cash. What maddened him was the wasted time and effort. Twirling his keys around his index finger, he thought he'd go inside and have a long moan to Elliott. He had the feeling she'd understand.

He stepped inside the house. "Fred?"

That was sure to get her arriving pronto, primed for battle. A good argument was just what he was in the mood for.

Silence.

"Fred? Are you there?"

The refrigerator started its mechanical hum. That was no substitute for a human voice. Then he remembered. She'd gone out.

He wandered into the kitchen, opened the fridge and closed it again. Maybe he should pour himself a whiskey. No, drinking on his own wasn't a good idea. But why not mosey along down to the pub? It was only a ten-minute stroll away. He wouldn't even have to take the car out again, and the temperature wasn't much below freezing. Unacknowledged was the fact that he really wanted to see Freddi in another setting.

Energized, he strode back to the entrance hall and set off.

FREDDI LEANED BACK and took a long, appreciative swallow of her third pint of beer. These local breweries were not bad at all. She put her mug down again. It landed too close to the edge and teetered.

"Ahem." Michael's voice had a funny edge to it. Freddi noticed the sound in spite of the increasingly rowdy background noise. She regarded her friend. Michael's bushy eyebrows arched like horizontal parentheses over his twinkling blue eyes. "Looks like we've got trouble."

Freddi frowned and looked over her shoulder, toward the bar. She couldn't see any signs of upheaval. "Is there a fight brewing?"

"We'll find out," Michael said, and sat forward in the easy chair. He looked up, way up.

Freddi swung back to stare. There stood none other than her boss, eyebrows clashing together, his expression thunderous. She took a quick swig of beer and made a sweeping movement with the mug.

"Hello, Jack. Meet Michael Pollack. My brother's friend from England."

Jack seemed to have forgotten all his nice new manners because he didn't respond.

She felt obliged to explain, though why she wasn't certain—it *was* her night off. "He's about to leave."

Michael rose, shook hands with Jack in an amiable fashion and nodded his confirmation. "Got a plane to catch." He turned to Freddi. "Sorry, sweetie, wish I could stay."

Freddi stood up. "I'll come outside with you."

"No, don't do that." Michael moved toward her and put his arm around her shoulder. "It's cold out there."

She gave him a hug and kissed his cheek. "It was a real treat to see you, Mike."

Biting her lip, feeling as though her last ally in the

whole world was leaving, Freddi watched him disappear out the door.

Jack snagged a nearby chair, turned it around and sat down. Arms over the back, chin on his hands, he scowled at Freddi.

"Sorry if I interrupted a tender love scene."

Freddi plumped back down into the easy chair, folded her arms and glared at him. "Don't be cynical, Jack. It doesn't suit you."

"And you're the expert on what suits me, are you?"

"I will be, soon enough."

That was a small part of what was bothering him at this particular moment. He didn't like feeling jealous and was amazed at the tide of rage that had risen in him when Freddi embraced Mike.

Freddi moved her legs, aware that Jack had his eyes on them.

"Let me buy you a drink," he offered.

"I don't think so." Already life had taken on a fuzzy edge.

"Why not?"

"I've got to go and see a man about a dog."

Jack lifted his chin and sat straight. "You do? I thought that was a male privilege."

"Equal opportunity, don't you know?"

"You don't know any men here, and I'm not ready to get a dog."

Freddi's brain seemed to have switched to slow. It took her a while to counter Jack's statement. At last she said, "I do know a man here," she stated.

"Who?"

She began a catalog. "I know all the delivery blokes, the FedEx fellas. I even met a fireman down the road while you were away." She fluttered her eyelashes. "He was dishier than George Clooney. All that fitness, full of testosterone."

He looked insulted. "I'm fit. And full of testosterone, too."

How did the conversation take this decidedly dangerous direction? She had to steer it off course. "Maybe, but you're my employer."

"So? It's your time off, isn't it?"

No denying that.

"You certainly don't look like my butler tonight."

His tone turned husky and sent a shiver down her spine. She stood, picked up her purse and walked toward the washroom, very aware of the fact that Jack was probably eyeing her back view. If there was an extra swing to her hips, well, that was entirely the fault of salsa class.

On her return, she was ultra conscious of how sexily she was dressed. With his eyes on her, she felt exposed, vulnerable. Little skittish darts prickled into her skin. In an effort to distract herself, she looked over to the dartboard. She should go across and join the game. Anything to escape Jack's ardent perusal.

"I approve of the getup." His gaze was hot on hers. "Why can't you wear those kind of clothes all the time?"

"They'd be a bit restricting in bed."

Oh hell, had she really said that? Freddi drew in a sharp breath, but those uncooperative words didn't roll themselves up and retrace their path back down her throat. Talk about a Freudian slip! She waited for Jack to respond, but he remained quiet.

At last he said, "Are you a woman who likes a challenge?" His eyes smoldered.

"Of course I am. Otherwise I wouldn't still be here."

He winked at her. How she wished he wouldn't do that. It caused instant meltdown.

"I'm in the mood for some fun. Wanna game?"

He nodded toward the darts.

"Yeah—" she flicked a hand in the direction of the board "—but there's a big crowd over there."

"How about a one-on-one?"

She could almost feel her pupils dilating, and her body seemed to have developed a tendency to turn into liquid. Hopefully that wouldn't be beer.

"Such as?"

"I don't know..." His eyes swept the room. "Yes, I do. Let's arm wrestle."

She bit her lip, eyeing his massive frame.

"What's the stake?" she asked suspiciously.

Jack appeared to ruminate. "You win, I'll take you out for dinner."

"Not enough."

"Also, I'll let you off wearing the heels."

Tempting. "And if you win?"

His smile was sensual, suggestive, and enough to have every lustful cell in her body come to quivering life. She breathed a noisy breath in and swallowed. Even her mind was salivating.

"*When* I win...then I'll buy you a couple of pairs of fishnet tights and have you wear them with the mini and the heels."

A small voice tried to protest that this was crazy, sure to make difficulties between a man and his butler. Before Freddi could back out, she and Jack were facing each other over a small round table. Already, he had his arm braced.

"Best of three?" he asked.

"All right," she replied, thinking that she'd have to get in quickly to seize the advantage.

His hand clasped hers. Forcing her mind to focus on her own body and not on his, she ignored the warm pressure that made her weak.

Jack commandeered a nearby patron to be the referee.

"Ready?" he asked.

They both nodded.

"Go!"

Freddi tensed her muscles as fast and as strongly as she could. Before Jack could even react, his arm was flat on the table.

After a stunned pause, he said, "I gave that one to you."

"Huh." She patted her hair. "I never suspected you'd be a poor loser, Jack."

Other patrons of the pub began to drift toward their table.

Once again, Jack and Freddi prepared for battle.

"Ready?"

They nodded.

"Go!"

Freddi tried her speed strategy again, but she wasn't too surprised to find it didn't work. Jack came back, squeezing and pressuring her. She paused to regroup and he caught her moment of weakness. Crash. Now it was her arm, flat back on the table.

"You want to take a break?" the referee asked, looking at Freddi with a glint in his eye. "Need something to drink?"

"No thanks." It was partly those somethings to drink that had landed her in this situation in the first place. That, and her own stupidity. Here she was, once again, locked in battle with Jack.

Vaguely she heard a spectator begin to chant, "Freddi, Freddi, Freddi," and soon the refrain was taken up by others. A few whoops and hollers sounded for Jack.

This time the match wasn't over in a flash. Both of them applied pressure, gripped harder. Trembling with effort, their locked hands and straining forearms swung this way, then that. In spite of all her bravado, Jack's arms were stronger than hers. Desperation had her digging in with her toes, straining her whole body, pushing harder. Impossible to keep this up for long.

She had to do something or he'd win and she'd be obliged to don fishnet tights and a miniskirt. No way would she parade around, providing him with titillation so he could go out and shag all his blond dates. That would be too humiliating. She should never have put herself in this predicament, especially as she wasn't prepared to lose. What should she do? She had to act, put him off somehow, and then go in for the kill.

Play dirty, said the puckish voice in her head.

Pain ran up the inside of her arm. She felt a tremor that signaled the onset of muscle failure. Her arm ached. This was all a big mistake. And just across the small expanse of round table, Jack was far too close. She could feel his body heat, breathe in the scent of his skin, of his breath. Was it her imagination, or was he leaning in closer? Closer than was strictly necessary?

His eyes were on her mouth. He *was* coming closer. Oh God, he was close enough to kiss. Oh yes. Kiss!

This was her chance! She could preempt him. Without a thought as to what she truly wanted, her mouth rose to meet his. She pressed a soft yet firm kiss on his lips. She heard the quick intake of his breath, sensed that this, while he was distracted, was the moment. With all her strength she pushed against his hand and slammed his arm down onto the table.

10

FREDDI HARDLY REGISTERED the whistles and "way to go's."

Victory, instead of feeling like a triumph, felt like a defeat. Her sex-deprived hormones had started frisking about, all perky and eager, and now they were pouting, accusing her of betraying them. Her body subsided into disappointment, and for a fleeting second she thought she saw the same in Jack's eyes.

"You little cheat."

She shrugged. "Snooze, you lose."

"We'll see about that."

"So, no fishnets for me."

Suddenly she was tired. Freddi brought the face of her watch up close to her eyes, then let her wrist fall. "After eleven! What happened to closing time?"

"This isn't England," Jack said. "We can drink longer than you Brits."

"Huh," she responded, but found no words to counter that.

Freddi got to her feet and swayed. All that arm wrestling had also affected her legs. They weren't behaving properly.

"Looks like it's time for you to hit the hay, *sweetie*." Jack stood. "I'll take you home."

Outside, the air was crisp enough to catch in her throat and make her cough. She hunched her shoulders, shoved her hands in her pockets and huddled her neck into her coat, wishing she'd brought her hat. Jack, on the other hand, seemed perfectly warm. His black leather jacket flapped unfastened, and his woolly scarf hung down.

He took her arm. "Hey, you're shivering."

She gave a trembling nod.

"Here, wrap this around you." He pulled the scarf from his neck.

They stopped. He twined the long length slowly around her neck and over her head. She stood quietly, watching him, waiting. Around them, the street, the city, the whole world was hushed. He put his hands on her ears, over the warm fabric, and tilted her face up to him. Very deliberately he lowered his head. Involuntarily, in invitation, her lids drifted down.

As cool as the snowflakes that fell on her the night she arrived, and as lightly tender, his lips touched hers. Even the streetlights seemed to glow more softly. A shuddering sigh moved through her and she rose on tiptoe. He angled his head more, wound his strong arms around her and took her mouth.

Jack's kiss. At last. After all the longing and fantasizing, the moment had come. A sudden nervousness made her meet his exploration hesitantly at first, then sensation took over.

His mouth was smooth and warm and just as marvelous, just as thrilling as she remembered. He tasted malty, the beer still lingering deliciously. He made her feel fizzy, right down to her pink-painted toenails. Freddi snuggled in closer, gave him more and lost herself in the bliss.

To Jack she was tempting, and hot enough to melt

the three-foot-high snowbank at the edge of the side-walk. Close by stood a convenient lamppost. But this was not the time, nor the place. Reluctantly, he lifted his mouth from hers, even though his baser instincts were cheering him on. Slowly he released her, and settled his hands on her waist.

Lids closed, Freddi stood, and swayed. Resisting the urge to kiss her again, Jack took her arm and turned toward home. By the time he'd taken a dozen steps forward into the cold night, his brain started to get some blood back. But he vowed that soon he would kiss her so thoroughly and so much that she wouldn't remember if this was day or night, April or May, England or Canada.

The kiss had given him something else to think about. He'd tasted her before. He was sure of it. Against all the rules of probability, she *had* been in his bed the night she'd arrived. However she'd gotten there, by whatever weird circumstances or crazy conjunction of planets, what his body remembered was true. She was delicious, she was addictive, and he had to have her. Soon. The memory had already tormented him far too long.

But not tonight. His own code of honor, put in words she herself might use, was that a gentlemen wouldn't shag a woman who was definitely tipsy.

JACK WAS DRESSED, breakfasted and ready to set off for the downtown office.

Freddi, uncertain now of how to react to him, was grateful for the structure they'd established. She went with him to the entrance and helped him on with the charcoal-gray overcoat. And then he stepped out of line. He turned toward her unexpectedly fast, and she found her hands resting against his chest. Feeling awkward, she lowered them and took a step back.

She saw Jack's throat bob, and then he stretched out his hand and touched the rose in her buttonhole. Mesmerized, all Freddi could do was stare up at him.

From the white petals, Jack's hand stroked upward until his knuckles rested against her cheek.

"How about a goodbye kiss?"

She blinked. "Oh...oh yeah. That would be, er, page forty-four of the buttling manual."

Jack chuckled and shook his head. "Okay. Maybe not normal buttling practice, but what about normal human practice, Freddi?"

She could risk giving him a quick peck on the cheek, couldn't she? Going up on tiptoe, she raised her mouth.

He swept her close and dived right in. Quick pecks were clearly far from Jack's mind. And why should Freddi want one anyway when he was being so very generous and giving her a bushel?

Freddi was right there with him. Beyond the faint flavor of minty toothpaste, she tasted his own unique flavor—as addictive as those chocolate truffles she indulged in occasionally. And now she allowed herself the indulgence of enjoying Jack's kiss. In the swirling, intoxicating sensations of taste and texture, the moving of mouths and tongues, she touched the essence, both physical and spiritual, of Jack Carlisle. She wanted to climb up him, be in him, with him.

A tiny but insistent electronic beep intruded. Jack's Palm Pilot. Reluctantly, he took his lips from hers.

"Early meeting. I must be on my way." His tone was low, husky.

She hitched in a breath and nodded. "Yes, Jack...I mean, sir."

An eyebrow lifted. "Just one instruction—I'll expect another one of those to welcome me home when I return."

Thoroughly unsettled, she drifted away from the entrance and dreamily began to clear the table.

At noon, the doorbell rang on Acorn Street. Freddi went to answer it. To her surprise, she saw a woman, tall, lovely, her strawberry-blond hair cut in a bob. Clutching onto her hand was a curly-headed cherub with wide, blue eyes.

Puzzled at the arrival time, but presuming this was the next candidate-in-line, Freddi asked, "Can I help you?"

With a friendly smile, the woman moved forward. "You're Freddi Elliott, right?"

Freddi nodded, her heart sinking. She could never compete with these two.

"I'm Louise. Is Jackie-boy back yet?"

Uh-oh, this sounded...serious.

"No. Mr. Carlisle's still at the office," Freddi said cautiously. "He doesn't usually get back till evening."

She was conscious of a crushing feeling of disappointment. Just when she thought—she was foolish if she'd thought something was developing between them.

Crouching down, the woman began unzipping the little girl's sky-blue snowsuit. "I know, but he promised me faithfully that he'd take the afternoon off." She tugged on one sleeve and off it came. The cherub held up her other arm. "He did say he might be late and that you'd take care of us and provide lunch."

Louise looked up with a warm smile. In spite of herself, Freddi couldn't help softening toward her. Meanwhile, her heart was hardening toward Jack.

"Er...yes. But I'm somewhat in the dark, here. Mr. Carlisle didn't tell me to expect anyone."

Standing up, Louise reached into the closet and retrieved a small hanger, one Freddi hadn't noticed before. "He didn't? Isn't that just typical? Too much on his mind, as usual, I suspect."

Whoever this woman was, she obviously knew Jack well and visited often. So why did he need the parade of blondes?

Freddi still felt at a loss. "Can you explain...?"

"Of course, honey! Forgive me, I was distracted, having to attend to Kim." The little girl blinked at Freddi and stuck her thumb in her mouth.

Her mother continued. "Jackie didn't tell you we were driving in from London? He promised to baby-sit so I could do some spring shopping."

Freddi folded her arms. She could feel the tension cramping the muscles in her neck. "No. He didn't."

"Brothers! I hope you've got one, so you can sympathize... Not that I don't adore Jack, of course. And so does Kimmie."

Freddi's shoulders slumped in relief. "I do have a brother, but I don't see him much anymore."

"Well, for the time being, you can share Jack."

Freddi thought about the ramifications of that. "I don't think so," she said. "But come on in, I'll put the kettle on and see what I can find for you to eat. Shall I cook Kim some vegetables?"

"That would be great."

"How old is she?"

"Sixteen months."

"She's too adorable for words."

The visitors followed Freddi into the kitchen.

"Would you like some orange juice?" she asked Kim.

The little girl nodded solemnly.

"I'll get it." Louise moved to the fridge. She poured the drink and then hitched the little girl up onto the counter to help her with the cup.

Freddi busied herself with preparing the vegetables and gathering ingredients for a light lunch. She became aware that Louise was watching her and turned to face the other woman.

Louise indicated Freddi's signature rose-in-the-buttonhole. "Nice touch."

Freddi smiled. "Thanks."

Louise set Kim down on the floor again. "I'll set the table," she offered. "You'll join us, won't you?"

"Oh no, it's—"

"Come on. I'd like the company and you have to eat too."

Soon the three of them were settled in the dining room. Little Kim picked up one of the bread soldiers Freddi had cut and buttered for her. She bit off the end and kept going.

"There's a good girl," Louise said.

Just then the front door burst open. Jack stepped inside, already half out of his coat.

"Hi, guys! Here I am, ready for the big event of my week."

With a small crow of joy, Kim wriggled off her chair

and went toddling forward to meet him. Jack opened his arms wide and swept her up, hugging her and kissing her curls.

"How's my favorite girl?"

Freddi stared at the picture they made. Something shifted inside her. His delight in the child made her heart go still.

She noticed the care he took as he carried Kim through, pulled out a chair for himself and sat down with her on his lap.

He smiled at his sister. "Great to see you both, Lou."

"You too, Jack...but Kimmie's busy eating lunch. You can cuddle her later."

"Aw...okay." He stood up. "Sorry, cookie, but Mommy knows best."

Kim laughed, patted his cheek with a chubby, outspread hand and, craning forward, pursed her lips for a kiss. Jack obliged, then carried her back to her chair.

Freddi, caught in a kind of waking dream, suddenly came to herself. She scrambled to her feet. Jack held up a hand.

"Stay right where you are. I'll get my own plate and cutlery."

On his return, he sat himself down next to her.

"How did you manage it, Lou?"

"What?"

"I've been trying to get Freddi to eat with me ever since she arrived. Without success."

Louise grinned. "I had help from the little charmer." She gathered up her plate, cutlery and cup. "You won't mind if I eat and run, will you?"

"Kimmie will console me, won't you, honey?"

Louise skipped out, blowing a kiss to them all.

Freddi wondered if they were in for trouble, if the little girl would cry. But all she did was blink when the door shut. Big eyes turned from Jack to Freddi and back again to Jack. She wriggled off her chair and went to him, holding up her arms. He picked her up and settled her on his knee.

Again, the sight of the small, feminine creature lying against Jack's chest sent an unexpected pang through Freddi. She wished...maybe she shouldn't look too closely at what she wished.

For the moment, Kim sat, content. Freddi got busy tidying the cutlery drawer and wondered how long the little girl would stay that way and how they would manage to keep her happy and entertained. However, after a few minutes she wriggled off Jack's lap and made her way across the room to a tallboy chest. She pulled open the bottom drawer and Freddi saw to her surprise that it was well stocked with toys. Kim reached for a soft doll, a small blanket and pillow, and began to play.

When at last she tired of her game, Jack, who'd moved to a couch set against one wall of the living room, set the magazine he'd been reading aside and found a picture book of nursery rhymes. Obviously knowing what was coming, Kim climbed up onto the couch and curled up next to him. Jack began to read. Freddi cast surreptitious glances in their direction, her heart twisting.

Hearing all her old favorites, she had to smile. It didn't seem so long ago that she had recited and read them to Matthew. She had to join in.

"Pat-a-cake, pat-a-cake baker's man," she sang, and clapped her hands this way and that.

Kim stared at her and began to imitate her actions.

Somehow the hours Louise was away flew by. Jack even managed to get Kim to take a little nap. She snuggled next to him on the couch while he read the newspaper. Then, when the sound and movement of his turning the pages obviously disturbed her, he put his own head back and closed his eyes.

Some time later, Kim on his hip, his hair rumpled, Jack appeared in the kitchen, where Freddi sat at her desk.

"I'd thought we'd take her to the park. Go feed the pigeons."

"We? You want me to come with you?"

"Please, Freddi. I presume Louise left the stroller?"

"Stroller? Yes, she did."

Freddi struggled with herself. She shouldn't go. But the sun was shining and the snow had all but melted. It would be good to have some fresh air, to get the blood running. On those grounds she decided it would be fine to join them.

She ran upstairs and took off her formal jacket, replacing it with a padded, lime-green anorak. Carefully she fitted the tab of the zipper into the slot, all the while picturing Jack's expression, thinking of the way he looked at Kim with a mixture of tenderness and delight. One day in the future, would he look at a child of theirs that way?

The zipper hissed as she drew it up. Get real, Elliott.

Outside, the air smelled different, carrying the hint of warmer days to come. Jack pushed the stroller. Walking next to him, Freddi was aware how the passersby must be perceiving them.

She continued to be struck by Jack's patience with

Kim. He acted as if he had all the time in the world to attend to her. It seemed he was happy to stop being the businessman for a while and enjoy the chance to be an uncle. In the park, Kim clapped her hands and laughed when he scattered bread crumbs for the birds. On chubby legs she tottered toward them, tried to give chase when they flew off. Jack smiled down at the child, so loving, so carefree.

Later, looking back over the day when she lay in bed that night, Freddi almost wished she hadn't glimpsed this softer, tender side of Jack. Almost.

JACK SAT DINING, a dish of steak with béarnaise sauce in front of him. Freddi poured him a glass of red wine.

"I wish you'd sit down, Freddi."

"Sorry, it's—"

"I know. Against the rules. Frankly, I don't set much store by rules."

He seized his steak knife and jabbed it into the meat.

"Jack! What on earth are you doing?"

"Me? I'm about to cut up my steak."

"Looks more like you're stabbing it. People will think you're a barbarian. First of all, one doesn't cut up the food first, but rather, as one goes along—using both the knife and the fork." She held the wine bottle closer to her, as if to restrain the words from forming in her larynx. But they popped out in spite of herself. "Do you think your coordination can handle that?"

Dark eyebrows rose. "I'll show you something of my coordination if you use that sarcastic tone, Freddi."

"No threats, Jack."

"I thought we were playing tit for tat."

His eyes flicked to her breasts and lingered for a few,

tantalizing moments. Their gazes locked in sexual promise.

"You'll break that bottle if you grip any harder. Remember, I've got the measure of you now."

She lifted her chin and turned to place the wine on the sideboard. When she started to move toward the kitchen again, a new movement from Jack caught her eye. He'd clasped his fork and was holding it upright in his fist.

"Jack, not like that! Didn't your mother teach you anything?"

He lowered the fork and looked at her with a wistful expression. "Not much. She died when I was ten."

Freddi pulled out the chair opposite him and sank onto it. "Oh, I'm so sorry. That must have been awful for you. Mummy died when I was fourteen, and that was bad enough." She rested her chin on her palm. "Did your father remarry?"

"Nope."

"That must have been hard."

"It was... What about you?"

"Oh, that was one of the good things about boarding school. Gave Matthew and me a kind of home from home."

"Your dad remarried?"

"Yes. Just a few years ago."

"And how is it with the new wife?"

"Neither of us took too kindly to our stepmother, especially as Charlotte the Shark's only twelve years older than I am."

Jack looked at her, understanding and sympathy in his gaze. She sighed, then realized his plate was almost clean. Time to resume her duties.

"Before I forget," Jack said, "I must tell you that the cleaning lady comes tomorrow."

Freddi pushed the chair close to the table, holding on to the back. "Lady who? Oh, you mean, your charwoman."

"Here they're called cleaning ladies."

She shrugged.

"You should get out of the way for an hour or two."

"I've got my dance class."

"Good." Jack stood up. "I'm off upstairs. There are some reports I need to read through tonight. But before I go, I'm going to collect on that rain check."

He came toward her, his eyes glittering.

"Has the weather changed?"

"Um."

His answer was delayed. Strong arms enfolded her. Firm fingers tilted her chin and he covered her mouth with his. This time their kiss was different, almost tender, lingering.

Reluctantly, Jack set her away from him and replied to her question. "I'm beginning to think it has," he said.

JACK STEPPED inside the house and heard music playing. He'd half extricated his arms from his jacket, when a movement in the living room caught his eye. Like a siren call he followed the rumbaish kind of beat, definitely Latin American. In the living room he found Freddi, clad in a bottom-skimming, scarlet flirty skirt, making swaying motions with her hips, while her legs flashed forward and back and her knees went around. She was lost in the movement and the music, completely absorbed, given up to the sensual rhythm.

His butler was concentrating so hard, she didn't even hear him come in, nor had she noticed the draft of cold air that wafted in with the opening of the front door.

Jack leaned against a pillar and folded his arms across his chest. So this was salsa, the sexiest dance on earth. He could corroborate that. The whole effect went straight to his groin.

Over the back of one chair lay a sweater. What would come off next? he wondered. The top would be good. He'd like to see her naked torso, a gold-link chain low on her hips...

Freddi was totally into it. She was the girl from Ipanema, the lovely with a hibiscus flower behind her ear, the most seductive woman in the world. Catching sight of Jack, she allowed her instincts to take over. Going with the lure of the music, she glided and swayed toward him. An extra wiggle crept into the movement of her hips.

He stood there, transfixed, while she got closer and closer. Now they were face-to-face, with only a few inches between their bodies. Jack shouldered himself away from the pillar, and at that moment she chucked him cheekily on his jaw and twirled away so that she was just beyond his grasp. Jack gave a growl.

In response, she let her shoulders sway and twirled about again. As she did so, her skirt flared up. Jack's eyes widened and he cocked his head to get a better view. Lids a little lower over her dark eyes, a small smile on her lips, she salsaed right back up to him. This time he shot out a hand and clasped her wrist.

Pulling her forward, he sneaked his other hand around her waist and drew her toward him. The music came to an end. She put her hands on his chest, holding him off.

"What are you doing here?" The words sounded breathless.

"Uh, this is my house...isn't it?"

"You said you'd be gone for two hours."

"So I hurried. And I'm glad I did."

"Yes. Well, er..." She blinked and stepped back.

He released her.

"What's the matter, Freddi? Cold feet?"

She nodded slowly. "Could be... Anyhow, I think I'd better go and change." She started heading to the stairs.

"Not for my benefit you don't have to. I'd be more than happy for you to stay like that, Fred."

"No, I need to go and change into something uncomfortable."

That made him laugh, and the sexual tension dissipated a little. Smugly, he realized he was getting somewhere with her. After all, she wasn't reacting to his shortening her name.

He went to his office and sat down at his desk. Then he leaned back in his chair and put his feet up.

In spite of his present relaxed position, he was a man of action. Certainly not afraid of going with his instincts. If he was to keep himself on track, he'd better put aside his suspicions that she might be spying for Simon and do something about getting her out of his system. He'd go about this in just the same fashion as he did business. He'd formulate a plan to get him exactly where he wanted to be.

And already an idea was starting to percolate.

11

JACK APPEARED in the kitchen the next morning after breakfast.

"I need to give you your instructions for the day."

"You're leaving now for the office?" Dishcloth in hand, Freddi turned toward him.

"In a few minutes."

Already in the habit of checking his appearance, she cocked her head to one side. Lips pursed, she looked him up and down.

An eyebrow quirked. "Do I meet with your approval?"

Did he ever. But it was her job to point out any lapses. She bit her lip and twisted the dishcloth. "Not quite."

Was that a glimpse of hurt she saw in his expression?

"It's the shoes." She blurted out the words, hating him to think she thought him lacking.

He looked down at his feet. "What's wrong with these? They're expensive, Italian and genu-wine leather."

"But they're dull."

"How far can you go with shoes?" He lifted one foot, regarded it and put it down again. Then he looked quizzically at Freddi. "Unless you want me to buy multicolor."

"What an awful thought." She twisted the dishcloth

between her fingers. "No, I mean, there's no shine. They're in need of a polish... I'll do that for you."

"I don't have time."

"It'll only take a minute or two, and if you want to look well groomed, your shoes should be impeccable." She threw the dishcloth at the sink and took a step toward him.

"I'm not going to take off my shoes!" He said it as if she'd asked him to strip for her.

Startled by his reaction, she took another deliberate step toward him and narrowed her eyes. "Why not?"

"Because...because I'll be late."

She helped him out. "And the boss will notice?"

"Yeah."

"I think...there's another reason." Standing in front of him now, she suddenly dropped to a crouch and grabbed his left foot. She seized the heel and tried to tug off the shoe.

He hopped away. "No, no, no!" His protest sounded melodramatic.

Freddi began to giggle.

This was like holding on to a lively grasshopper. Just about impossible. Laughing, she gave up, and fell backward. Jack squirmed away, and, grabbing on to the handle of the fridge, just managed to save himself from landing on his duff.

Hands on hips, he looked down at her. "Is this Elliott, the dignified butler?"

"No. It's her alter ego, Fred."

With laughing eyes, he bent down to help her up. "Ah, Freddikins. Pleased to meet you."

"No, Jack, never say that."

His smile faded and he sent her an inquiring glance.

"It's always 'How do you do,'" she explained.

He stuck his tongue in his cheek. "Yeah, maybe that's better. Pertinent in these circumstances."

She wasn't sure that he meant what she thought he meant. She swallowed. Time to get on with her duties.

"Look, no need to take your shoes off, although I can't imagine what you've got to hide. A hammer toe maybe? An ingrown toenail? Or maybe an extreme case of the dreaded lurgs."

"What's that?"

"I don't know...athlete's foot?"

"No."

"Aha!" She grinned. "I know. A hole in your sock."

That was almost a pout she saw. Biting her lip to stop her smile, she grabbed the rung of the chair by the built-in desk and swung it around.

"Sit here, and I'll polish them for you right now. On the foot."

"Okay." Jack gave his crisp nod and settled himself.

Freddi located the hand crafted wooden caddie she'd equipped with cloths, brushes and polishes of various colors. Kneeling in front of Jack, she set the box on the floor next to her, prepared to give him a good shine. With Jack's foot resting on her thigh, his body so close to hers, she soon began to feel hot. Even if she was wearing three layers of clothing—stockings, skirt and apron—and there was Jack's sock plus the sole of his shoe, it might as well have been his bare foot on her naked thigh. She bent her head, hoping that Jack wouldn't notice her flushed cheeks.

"I think—" his voice held a note of amusement "—that shoe's had enough attention. Unless you want to buff the top layer off."

"Oh." She gasped, and stopped.

Jack withdrew his foot, and Freddi looked up. What she saw at eye level didn't do anything for her composure. Hastily, she curled her fingers around his other ankle and brought that shoe forward. She set to work, determined to keep her focus where it should be. But that naughty focus was determined to stray. How would it be, she wondered, if she moved forward, unzipped him and gave a certain part of Jack's gorgeous anatomy a bit of a spit and polish?

Concentrate on the task at hand, Freddi. Or rather, at foot. Force yourself to think of other things. Not Jack. Not sex.

Jack spoke again. There was a different note in his voice.

"I'll be entertaining tonight, Elliott."

Brush in hand, she stiffened. *Now* he called her Elliott, just when she was getting warm gooey feelings when he called her Freddi.

"Yes, sir." She tried to make her voice prim, professional.

"This is someone special. We're already on rather familiar terms."

"What's her name, if you don't mind my asking? It's useful for me to know."

"Her name? Er, um, Abby Dobon... Anyhow, tonight's the night."

She sat back on her heels. Did he mean what she thought he meant? "Very good, sir."

Jack said nothing more. She bent to her task and this time she cut it as short as possible. Freddi knew she should ask for specific instructions, but she found herself reeling from a flood of emotions—fury, jealousy, disappointment that Jack should overlook her. She felt invisible, and for the first time wished she didn't have to stay in uniform. Part of a butler's task was to maintain a kind of impersonal anonymity, and the formal, unchanging dress code contributed to that. Dammit. Why couldn't Jack see *her* instead of Elliott? Hadn't their kisses had the same electrifying effect on him as they had on her? How ironic, at first she'd wanted him to see Elliott instead of Freddi, and now that he was doing exactly that, she wished it would be the other way around.

"Thanks, that's good." Jack put his foot back on the floor. He continued to watch her.

Slowly she began to pack away the shoe-shining stuff. "Would you like me to leave for the evening?"

"No. I need you here."

She folded the soft yellow duster, making sure the corners were precisely aligned. Then she tucked it in the box and stood.

Jack looked up at her. "A butler is supposed—or rather, trained—to be discreet, isn't hee-shee?"

"You sneezed, sir?" she asked jeeringly.

"No, I asked a question. But if I *had* sneezed, I would have expected you to bless me."

Shoe caddie in hand, she lifted her nose. "I can't do that."

His eyebrows rose. "Not among your many admirable talents?"

"Not just at the moment, sir. If you want blessing, you'd better go to church."

"I'll think about it." Jack clapped his hands on his knees and stood up. "Ahem. To repeat my question—" and he asked it again.

"Of course, sir. Discretion is imperative."

"Great." He moved closer to her, stretched out his hand and began stroking the petals of the white rose in her buttonhole. "Because I'm harboring certain hopes for tonight."

His fingers hovered a little above her breast. She fought to keep her breathing even, at the same time wondering why he seemed determined to tease her.

"Yes?" Up till now she'd had no indication that Jack could be cruel, but his emphasis on his potential score for the evening was hard to take.

"The thing is..." He took the caddie from her and stowed it in the broom closet. She waited for him to continue.

He turned to her and ran a finger around the inside of his shirt collar. "I want you to set the seduction scene for me—soft music, low lights, flowers—you know the kind of thing."

This was too much. She picked up the feather duster and began ostentatiously flicking at the top of the cabinets. She dusted with a fury, stirring up dust bunnies and winding up her temper.

"That's not in the buttling manual, sir."

Fanning his fingers in front of his mouth. He sneezed.

Silence.

"Uh, excuse me." He sniffed a couple of times, then continued, "I have a suggestion... Why don't you use your feminine intuition and please yourself? Pretend you'll be entering this scenario." Palm downward, he made a wavy gesture. "Imagine a romantic dinner, tastes, sights and sounds that might put you in the mood."

"The mood for *what*, sir?" Did he have to labor the point like this?

"Think of Austin Powers again, and you'll be on track."

On that note, Jack turned. Then he looked back at her.

"No appearing in the undertaker outfit, see?"

She heaved a sigh of exasperation. "The rules—"

"Won't prevent you from at least wearing the miniskirt."

And with that last imperative, he strode off. No chance she was going to follow him and help him on with his leather jacket. She jammed her fists onto her hips when she heard him whistling a jaunty tune. "I Feel Good," if she wasn't mistaken, although it wasn't easy to be sure. The front door clicked shut. She was on her own.

Sabotaging thoughts exploded in her head. What could she do to put this woman off? Maybe organize a heavy meal. How about something British? A steak and kidney pie with mashed potatoes, green peas and turnips, followed by a steamed suet pudding—spotted dick maybe—and Stilton cheese. Heavy red wines. Also, to spike the ambience, she could spread a few cactuses around in strategic places. As a last resort, she could apple-pie Jack's playground—his bed. She hadn't done that since she and Tabby had targeted Geraldine Featherstonehaugh, their common enemy at boarding school.

Finding herself at one of the long living-room windows, Freddi looked down at the patch of garden. The small square was no longer covered with white. All the snow had melted, revealing an expanse of dreary

brown grass and some sticklike, bare shrubs. She knew
exactly how the earth felt, as if the promise of spring
were nothing but an illusion.

LATER, FREDDI had everything ready. The excellent
home caterer she'd discovered had delivered the foil-
wrapped dishes. All she had to do was place them in
the oven and assemble the starter course.

She'd taken Jack's words to heart, conjuring up all
her own preferences and dreams and using them to set
the scene for the evening. Earlier, by throwing herself
wholeheartedly into her salsa class, she'd danced off
her anger and disappointment. She imagined herself
with the promised bonus, taking a holiday in Brazil
maybe, feeling free, uninhibited and feminine. She
didn't need Jack.

Nevertheless, having changed her attitude and
thrown herself into the task, when he came downstairs
she found herself staring, tempted to change her mind.
Attired in an ivory silk shirt and black dress pants, he
was enough to make her breath catch in her throat.
Clean shaven, with his dark hair gleaming, he looked
wonderful, but still somehow untamed. Suddenly she
felt sexy in her miniskirt, and very aware of her lace-
topped stockings, the bare flesh of her thighs above
them. She tugged at her hem, making sure it hung
properly.

Tonight there was a kind of pent-up energy about
Jack. Usually he was the epitome of cool. Now he
paced up and down. From time to time he shot out his
left arm and glanced at his watch.

"Relax, Jack. What does it matter if this Abby Dobon

is late? Even if she doesn't turn up, would that be so terrible?''

He paused, shoved his hands in his pockets and began, ''It's a guy thing, Freddi. Sexual rejection doesn't do much for the ego.''

She gave a sniff. So far, apart from his uncertainty about social graces, she'd seen nothing to make her think Jack's ego was under any kind of threat, especially not a sexual one.

Ten minutes later, he was still wandering around. Suddenly he seemed to come to a decision. He drew his hands out of his pockets and approached her.

''Light the candles, please, Freddi.''

She kneeled in front of the coffee table, all too conscious of him watching her light the half-dozen tea lights in midnight-blue glass holders. Carefully she held the match to the first, then the second. As she did so, she imagined how it might feel to be the object of Jack's desire. One by one the wicks caught and began to flicker and glow.

She glanced his way. For the moment at least, all of his attention was on her. In fact, he was looking at her as if she *were* the object of his desire. Her heart kicked against her breastbone. If only it were true. Knowing the way he made her feel, the wild excitement that his kiss ignited in her, made her long for so much more.

While she was busy with the fifth candle, he went over to the wall and turned the dimmer switch.

''Now, let's hear the music, Freddi—whatever you've selected to get you in the mood.''

''Get *me* in the mood?'' She went still, brain on shutdown, body on start-up. The match flame grew bigger, closer, hotter. She blew it out just before her fingers got burned.

"Slip of the tongue," he said, coming over and sitting down on the couch, right opposite her. "Or, better said, wishful thinking."

Freddi was thinking about Jack's tongue sliding, and almost missed the second part of what he said. Had she heard aright? Fingers trembling, she struck another match and held it to the last candle.

"Very good." His voice was soft. "Now don't forget the fire."

How could she forget the fire when she was this close to him?

She lit the scrunched-up newspaper and watched the flames licking upward, catching on the kindling. She saw the logs begin to spark and glimmer. And still she was aware of his intent gaze.

"...and the music," Jack reminded her.

If this continued, she'd soon betray herself. She shifted and stood.

The sound system had been primed. A stack of CDs waited to send romantic rhythms and beguiling melodies into the air. She hit the play button. What a pity she couldn't hit Jack's play button.

The smoky tones of a torch singer began to waft and swirl through the living-room area until the swelling, rippling, sexy tide of sound filled every corner of the room. Jack slouched deeper into the cushions of the couch, his eyes glittering.

He looked so tempting, sprawling there, that Freddi longed to drop into his lap and have her way with him. Reminding herself that his date du jour was likely to appear at any moment, she fled.

In the domestic sanctuary of the kitchen, she looked around for something to keep herself occupied, away from Jack. Might as well put the finishing touches to the meal. On the counter, two white plates waited, ready to receive the first course—a somewhat updated version of avocado ritz.

Holding the weight of the globular fruit in one palm, wondering how Jack would feel if she cupped him like that, she cut the avocado in half and carefully removed the pit. The acidy-appley green would look wonderful on the white china. She peeled back the skin, all the while appreciating the texture of the flesh, so smooth and dense and rich, slightly slippery against her fingers. After cutting the fruit into even slices, she spread them into a fan shape. As she did so she mused on what it might be like, how it would feel, to make love with Jack.

She sighed.

From the fridge she took the container of shrimp in cocktail sauce, and from the pantry the bottle of Tabasco. The touch of red chili would add a little spice.

Freddi dipped her finger into the container and popped some of the sauce in her mouth to taste. Now, if she were the date, she wouldn't need any added spice. Just to enjoy Jack's complete attention would be enough to set her on fire.

Hot thoughts had Freddi staring into space as she savored the appetizer. The flavor of the smooth creamy sauce teased her taste buds. The bite of red chili pepper made her tongue tingle.

A tall figure appeared in the doorway.

She started, drew her finger out of her mouth and licked her lips guiltily.

Hands deep in his pockets, Jack strolled into the kitchen. She turned toward the counter and looked down at the plates, wondering just exactly what she'd been about to do. The fact that he was now standing behind her banished her concentration. Aware that he was looking over her shoulder, leaning over her, she swallowed again and reminded herself that, if she wanted to stay in the land of the living, she had to breathe.

"Checking on the flavor?" he asked in his teasing voice.

She bit her lip and closed her eyes. He was so close she could feel his body heat, smell the subtle, lemony fragrance of his after-shave, feel his breath on her cheek.

Mouth still tingling with the flavor of shrimp sauce, she nodded.

"Can I have a taste?"

Her pulse tripled. She hitched in a breath. *Anytime, Jack, anytime.* To stop herself from jumping him, she decided to go on the attack. That might be the best defense against her impulses.

"Jack, you should take your hands out of your pockets."

"I have to keep them there."

"Why?"

His dark eyes intent on her, he stepped back, slowly withdrawing his hands.

"Because otherwise...otherwise they'll do naughty things."

"Naughty things?" she echoed faintly.

All at once the mood had changed. She'd never seen

him quite like this before. It sent chills down her spine. She was all too aware of his nearness.

"What do you mean? Steal some of the shrimp?"

"No, I mean, reach for you." He stretched forward, put his hands on her shoulders and turned her toward him. "Like this."

Then she was in his arms, gathered up into his embrace, engulfed in him. All she knew was the feel of his warm, strong arms encircling her, his taut chest, stomach and thighs pressed closely against her. At last.

His mouth melding with hers had her wanting more. Oh, but his kiss was potent. The taste, the smell, the feel of him filled all her senses. Never before had she known what it meant to be so swamped in sensation that all her surroundings disappeared into nothing. Jack was everything.

He lifted her so that she sat on the edge of the counter. Her arms twined around his neck and she reached for another kiss, for Jack, willing to let him take her wherever he would.

Slowly he released her. Large, warm hands stroked down her front to her waist, where her jacket was fastened closed. His fingers slipped the button through the buttonhole and parted the two sides. Her skin tingled as she felt his caress moving upward, barely grazing her breasts, up to her shoulders. She shrugged so that the garment began to fall. Grasping the end of one sleeve, he helped her out of it. Next, Jack discarded her vest and undid the tie.

She sat silent, breathless, allowing him the freedom to undress her, enjoying the tantalizing knowledge that she would soon be naked from the waist up. His knuckles were gentle against her as he undid the shirt buttons. Her eyes closed and her head fell back at the exquisite sensation. Then he opened the sides of her blouse and lifted it away from her shoulders. She saw his gaze fix on the pale swell of her flesh, the rosy pink tips. This time his hands glided over her and his fingertips began to caress her breasts, lightly stroking the sensitive nipples. Excitement and exhilaration gushed through her, flooding her with a frenzy of thrills and delight that had her gasping and sighing.

But there was something buzzing around in the back of her brain, an annoying gnat that prevented her complete abandon. This wasn't what she'd been expecting. Suddenly it all clicked into place—Jack's edginess, his asking her to please herself. There was no date except her. She had choreographed the scene for her own seduction. And his.

She decided to make sure.

"Jack." Her voice came out sultry, low. "What if your date arrives?"

12

ONE ARM REACHED behind her, so that her breasts thrust against him. The rhythm of his fingers on her flesh continued. She dug her nails into his skin.

"What date? No date." Dipping his head, he began to kiss and lick. "Only you," he mumbled.

That was what she'd needed to hear.

When at last he lifted his mouth, he said, "I've been hungry for you...for too long."

"Yes." The faint sound of agreement whispered from her lips.

Through the drugging fog of her desire she felt a feather-light touch stroking up her thigh, higher, higher. Her short skirt and satin tap panties made her easily accessible to him. His hands paused when his fingers felt the lacy tops of her stockings. He drew back a little, looked down at her and groaned.

"If I'd known—" his voice was hoarse "—that you were wearing these, I would have torn your clothes off days ago."

She shifted, opening herself to him. His fingers began to explore, his touch intimate, teasing, until he began to probe, slowly, rhythmically.

Desperate for more, she pushed at his shoulders. Then all was turmoil and frantic tugging, stroking, pushing as they fought to get at each other. She undid his zipper and freed him, holding his silky, straining erection in just the way she'd imagined.

He stilled. She heard him catch his breath and swallow. Somehow she read his intention. Although her body was clamoring for him, frantic for completion, she had to be practical. She wrenched her mouth away from his. "Jack! Wait! We're not prepared."

He fumbled in his pocket. "Oh yes, we are." She heard the foil packet rip. "I'm not waiting. Not more than another two seconds."

He was true to his word. The moment came. Freddi clutched onto Jack's shoulders, gripping tight with her fingers as he fitted himself to her. Slowly and deliberately he slid into her. She squeezed her eyes shut, savoring the sensation of him filling her, clinging to the knowledge that this was Jack. He was hers. At last.

She shuddered at the exquisite sexiness, her brain, her body absorbing the unbelievable thrill.

He began to move, his rhythm in tune with the music that wafted in from the living room. She sank into mindless delectation. Jack made her body tremble, and come alive. He made her heart weak. She wrapped her legs around him, urging him on; and felt the hard surface behind her.

"Jack!" she moaned. "This is crazy. There's a fire in the fireplace. Why are we in the kitchen?"

"Fantasy," he panted. "The counter...just...the right...height. Fire...later."

She hitched in a shuddering sigh. "Later," she gasped. "If...I'm still...on the earth."

The tension, the ecstasy, built with the driving rhythm. Higher and higher he took her.

Freddi felt the urgency increase toward the final

buildup. She was floating gloriously, yet at the same time completely absorbed, focused on her body's sensations. Jack threw his head back and froze. She clutched at him, digging her fingers into the silk of his shirt. Then came the inner throbbing of his explosion—from him, into her, setting off waves of release, the pulsing of ultimate pleasure.

Jack shuddered out a long sigh. ''Ah, Freddi.'' He lowered his head, his forehead resting against hers. ''Wow.''

Slowly, she came to herself. Her body went limp. She was all undone, in disarray, having taken all sorts of lovely liberties with her employer...and vice versa. Gradually, she lifted her eyelids.

Jack looked at her. A slow, satisfied grin spread across his face.

Freddi slid off the counter, thinking that, if their little episode had been vice, it certainly felt incredibly good.

Nearby, the avocado ritz lay undisturbed. How surprising that it hadn't rearranged itself during the action. She certainly felt rearranged, as if Jack had added a missing dimension to her body and soul, as if her life had just been enhanced, made more vivid.

He picked up one of the plates, lifted a shrimp and held it out to Freddi. Obligingly, she opened her mouth. The sauce-coated seafood was tangy on her tongue. She savored it, swallowed and licked her lips. Jack blew out a breath, gave her a quick kiss, then helped himself.

Jack continued to feed her, now a shrimp, now a slice of smooth avocado, in between taking mouthfuls himself, until both plates were empty.

''What's that delicious smell? I wonder.'' He opened

the oven door and checked inside. "Oh my...can't let all your preparations go to waste." He shut the oven and looked at her. "Why don't you go sit by the fire? I'll bring you a plate of food."

This was turning the tables. She liked it, but she wasn't dressed for the occasion. "I need to go upstairs and, er, find something else to wear."

"No way! Here." He picked up her white shirt and held it out for her. She slid one arm in and then another and felt his hands settle on her shoulders. They slid down to fasten one button.

"Will that keep you warm enough?" He turned her to face him and smiled down at her. "The sight of you wearing only the shirt and the black stockings will keep me cooking."

"Maybe I should take them off." Teasingly she fingered the lacy top that clung to her right thigh.

Jack's eyes narrowed and he swallowed. "Nuh-uh. That's going to be my privilege...a little later...I'll roll them down, very slowly, and then work my way up again."

Her senses stirred at the thought. The oven began to ding.

"Uh-oh. Up to temperature. Looks like I'd better take the hint and build up my strength... Go ahead, Freddi. Relax on the couch. I'll be with you, shortly."

Jack was a man of his word. They snuggled together on the couch and enjoyed the food, their mood leisurely and content as they chatted aimlessly. After dessert, Freddi went to the kitchen to get a drink of water. Some crème brûlé was left, so she picked up the dish.

Back in the living room, she held it up and asked Jack, "Would you like a second helping?"

His eyes glittered. "I most definitely would. Come over here, Fred, and forget the custard."

Understanding was instant, and so was her response. Her body began to melt. As she moved back toward the couch, Jack slid down. He pulled her onto his lap.

"Now it's time to keep my promise."

A warm hand curved around her stocking-clad thigh.

"Oh," she sighed.

His fingers began teasing their way upward. They toyed with the lace at the top of her leg, from the outside to the inside. Freddi could hardly breathe. Then slowly, just as he'd said he would, he drew the flimsy stocking downward and off, away from her toes. Amazing how she felt naked all over again.

She closed her eyes as Jack worked his magic, stroking up, making little circles behind her knee, taking his time to get back to where he'd started. Sweeping strokes, tiny tickles. By the time he got to the top, Freddi was trembling with want. And then he began giving the other leg the same attention.

A log shifted in the fireplace. Jack glanced at the smoldering ashes.

"Uh-oh, we don't want to cool off too much, do we? Time to put on a couple of new logs and stoke up the fire."

Weak with desire, Freddi couldn't imagine needing any more heat. What she needed was Jack. But maybe a little breathing space would be good. She slid off his lap and knelt on the hearth. First, she took the poker and rearranged the burnt logs. Flames flickered to life.

Next to her was the wood she'd stacked earlier. She chose two logs and carefully placed them on top.

"You do that very well," he whispered.

"Putting logs on?" Already she could feel the increased warmth.

"No, stoking the fire."

She was watching to see that they didn't roll, when she heard Jack move off the couch.

Warm hands touched her shoulders and peeled back the shirt she was wearing. Closer he came, so that she leaned back against him, felt his skin against hers, his chest firm and strong. His chin lay on her shoulder and for a while he kept still, saying nothing, just watching the play of the firelight on her skin. Small kisses crept up the side of her neck, wide hands stroked upward, teasing her breasts.

Growing impatient, Jack stretched behind him and pulled two cushions onto the floor. They lay down in front of the rekindled fire.

Leisurely lovemaking; warmth from without, heat within. Now that their initial ardor had been tempered they took the time for lingering caresses, gently exploring kisses. Passion flickered, then flamed, sending sparks of desire shooting through Freddi's body.

"Come to me, Jack," she pleaded.

Ever eager to please, he rose above her, his broad shoulders highlighted in the undulating firelight.

Playfully, she pushed at his chest. "Lie back, I'm going to have my way with you," Freddi said, her voice low and throaty.

Her wish was his command. Jack was happy to oblige. Now it was her turn to tease, and she did just that, scratching little circles over his chest, working her way downward, paying attention to the soft skin of his lower abdomen, the smooth angle where his thighs began, touching and kissing everywhere except the place that waited, straining for her touch. Then at last, she covered him with her mouth.

He closed his eyes, surrendering to the ravishment. Time and place had no meaning. Only Freddi and he existed as she wound him tighter and tighter. His breath came out in a whoosh. "Can't...stand that...too much longer, whew...or you'll miss out on...the main event."

At last she lowered herself onto him and began to take her pleasure. He looked up at her flushed cheeks, her rapt expression, her slumberous eyes. She was beautiful.

Afterward, they lay together on the couch. Tenderly, contentedly, Freddi stroked his back.

Her heart stirred. This elation she felt, which was a kind of peace, a certainty that all was right with her world, this was far more than the result of physical thrills. Over the last little while she'd come to know Jack, to appreciate his sterling qualities. They'd had fun together, made wonderful love together. So what did it all mean? The certainty was born and spread through her. What she had sensed, and shied away from that very first moment when she'd seen Jack, looming tall in his doorway, had now occurred. She was in love with the man. Totally and completely besotted.

She swallowed. Steady on, Elliott, don't panic here, and above all, don't let on. Even if she was flooded with love for him body and soul, to Jack this might be only an interlude, having no lasting impact on his life or his deeper feelings. It could be just an attraction, brought on by proximity. She must hold back until she was sure.

"Woman, that was..."

Her eyes opened. She managed to smile at him. "What?"

"A surprise."

"A *surprise?*" Did he mean the experience had been as extraordinary for him as it had been for her?

"Yes. A phenomenal, whack-you-over-the-head, astonishing surprise."

He propped his head up with his hand, one elbow digging into the cushion as he smiled back at her. The other hand tenderly curled a strand of hair back behind her ear.

"You didn't think it would be this good?" she asked.

"I couldn't ever have imagined it, not even in my best, wildest fantasies. Of course—" he began to stroke her cheek, her chin, her lips "—the kiss should have been a clue, but I somehow suspected you'd be a lot more inhibited."

She licked her lips. "It's that British-chick thing, is it?"

"Yeah—snotty and uptight. Boy, how wrong can a man be?"

"Seems to me you found out just exactly how wrong a man can be—thanks to Abby Dobon."

"Who?"

"You know, Abby Dobon. The blonde you were expecting." She opened her eyes wide, showing she knew about the setup.

"Er, yes. Her." Jack grinned. "Thanks to good old Abby." Bracing himself on his wrists, he pushed himself up and away from Freddi. He sat back up on the couch. "Maybe we should have a toast to good ole Abby—and us, of course. I'm thirsty. How about you?"

"Hmm. I could do with something cool."

"Stay right there. I'll get some drinks."

Sipping at the frosty contents of their glasses, they watched the flames subside into embers. Jack kept his arm looped over Freddi's shoulders and played with her neck.

"I've never seen anything as fine as your skin...the creamy color, the scent."

He pressed a kiss onto her forehead, turning her a little. They stayed like that. Soon the warmth, the satiation, made Freddi drowsy. Her eyes drifted shut.

"Tired?" Jack asked.

"No, just sleepy and relaxed. I don't want to move for the next five days."

"Doesn't a good big bed sound appealing?"

She smiled. "Yeah."

Jack scooped her up into his arms and headed for the bedroom.

There they lay content, Freddi with her head resting in the crook of Jack's arm. She ran a hand over the bed linen, enjoying the feel of the fine fabric.

"I have to tell you, I really approve of your sheets."

"Thank my sister. They were a housewarming gift from her... Been in them before, have you?"

Lulled by the postcoital mood, Freddi answered, "Yes, I—" Her jaw dropped as she realized the implications of her answer.

"Aha! At last!" Jack pulled her closer and tangled his legs with hers. "Proof of what I suspected."

"So you knew."

"I wasn't sure."

She snuggled into him, and stroked a hand down his flat stomach, then settled it on his waist.

"I mean," Jack continued, "I didn't expect my butler to crawl into bed with me."

"It was a mistake."

"I didn't think so. I thought it was the best thing that had happened to me in weeks, and it gave me a clue. Without that, I would never have suspected that my straitlaced butler could be so passionate and uninhibited."

"Maybe it was all for the best then." She yawned and her eyelids closed. Before his very eyes she went into her dormouse act. Jack smiled tenderly and followed her into dreamland.

THE SOUND of the phone ringing brought Freddi out of a deeply contented sleep. Eyes shut, she licked her lips, cleared her throat and said loudly, "A-B-C-D-E-F-G," hoping that would remove the croak from her voice.

"Good morning. Mr. Carlisle's residence."

"Freddi! Is that you?" The voice boomed in her ear. "How are you, my gel?"

She glanced at Jack. He lay on his stomach, the beauty of his back revealed to her. She admired his shoulder blades, the pattern of his muscles, the way his spine marked a line between the curved symmetry of his buttocks. His head was turned away from her, his dark curls in disarray.

He began to stir. For the second time in her life she was grateful he was a heavy sleeper. Especially as Uncle Avery was still of the conviction that it was necessary and helpful, when calling long distance, to be brief and to raise the voice.

"Fine, thank you." She extricated herself from the sheet, stood up and carried the phone to the other end of the room.

"Is that nephew of mine up and about?"

She'd better not think of Jack being up. "Yes, he is indeed."

"Put him on the line, then."

"I'll have to call him from upstairs," she lied. "Please hold on a minute." She covered the earpiece with her hand.

Jack was awake now. He scraped his hands down over his face, squeezed his eyes shut, then opened them wide. "Help! Hearing you recite the alphabet like that made me think I was back in grade school." He held out a hand for the phone. "What's this all about?"

"It's Mr. Carlisle," Freddi whispered.

Jack gave his head a little shake, as if trying to wrench his mind away from sex and on to other, more mundane matters. Both he and Freddi heard exactly what Uncle Avery said.

"I'm at Heathrow, my boy. About to board the aircraft for Toronto. I expect to see you in some—uh—seven hours or so."

"No problem. I'll be there to meet you." To his credit, Jack didn't even stutter.

"Glad to hear that. And shall we say, dinner tonight?"

"It will be my privilege—" Jack waggled his eyebrows suggestively at Freddi "—to entertain you, sir."

Freddi grinned at Jack and gave him an approving thumbs-up.

He hung up and ran a hand through his darling dark locks, which had grown somewhat unkempt in the weeks she'd been with him.

"You heard?"

Freddi nodded.

"Why now?" He shook his head. "I'm not ready for this."

She lay down on the bed next to him and traced the tattoo on his arm, thinking that a lion rampant had been an appropriate choice. He reached for her and fitted her against his long body.

Smiling tenderly, she said, "Yes, you are. You'll do fine."

He was the man who'd unshackled her inhibitions, who'd boosted her into the stratosphere. But now it seemed they'd have to get him tamed down in the next little while. What a pity.

"Don't worry, I'll take care of everything. Will you dine here?"

"No, downtown would be best. Uncle Avery will need to go to bed early. He'll probably want to look at the office, then I'll take him to the hotel. We'll do the impressive dinner tomorrow."

"So all you have to do is get yourself looking presentable."

"How'm I going to do that?" he asked glumly.

"The usual way—shower, shampoo, shave. And dress in the suit, shirt and tie I got you for your trip to New York." She marched two fingers up the center of his chest. "But before you put on your formal clothes, you should go for a haircut."

He pushed his arms out and upward in a gigantic

stretch. She took the opportunity to admire his shapely torso.

"Okay. The barber's close by. I can be outta here and back with you in forty-five."

"No. You'll want something more recherché, as well as a manicure. I've got the name of a place in Summerhill."

Jack let out a long-suffering sigh. "I had no idea the English were so into personal grooming."

"Remember, appearances give your first and strongest impression. After that, you can demonstrate your charming personality. I presume your uncle's already aware of your business acumen."

She was playing with the dark tufts of hair on his chest. Her fingers twined and stroked, and, all on their own, without her giving them any instructions, began to follow the arrowing path downward. She felt Jack's body go on full alert. His arm cradled her, his hand gripped her shoulder and squeezed. At the same time as he lowered his head to her, she lifted her mouth to his.

Reluctantly she pulled herself out of the kiss and pushed at his shoulders. "I should get up and get started."

"Exactly what I was thinking."

She gave a gurgling chuckle. "There's no time."

"True. No time like the present," he said, his actions confirming the words.

JACK WAITED at the airport in Toronto. He sat in a too-small, molded plastic chair, a newspaper spread open in front of him. He drummed his fingers on his thighs, glad that Freddi had taken the clear varnish off his nails. She'd been horrified to see they'd been painted, and vocal as to what Uncle Avery would think. How cozy it had been with her holding his fingers, letting him cop a feel while she cleaned away the evidence of the manicurist. How was he ever going to keep his mind off her?

Glancing up at the board, he saw that twenty minutes had passed since the plane arrived. Uncle Avery was sure to travel first-class, which meant his bags would be among the first to be taken off and he could well appear at any moment.

With the newspaper tucked under his arm, Jack stood and shouldered his way through the crowd until he found a convenient spot to watch and wait.

The gray-glazed doors opened and several travel-weary passengers with mounds of luggage and relieved expressions came through. Some of them looked around, bewildered. None of them was familiar, as yet. Jack breathed in and wiped his hands on his trousers. No need to be nervous. He could handle Uncle Avery. Freddi had coached him well. He'd couched her well. Dammit, Jack, put last night out of your mind.

The doors opened again. A porter pushed through a trolley of luggage, and next to him, bushy eyebrows all awry from his journey, bustled his uncle. Jack took one step forward then froze. A couple of feet behind, slim and elegant, his longish, sandy-blond hair flopping over one eye, walked his unbeloved cousin Simon.

13

HIS NEMESIS, all Britishly elegant in gray slacks and a navy blazer with gold buttons, an armorial-looking badge adorning one pocket, was here in North America. What a pity he couldn't confine Simon to the small, wet, miserable island he came from. Why did he always have to stick his nose in where he wasn't wanted?

Doing his best to tamp down his annoyance, Jack waved his newspaper. Uncle Avery responded, and the porter swung the trolley in Jack's direction.

Recalling Freddi's comprehensive instructions, he summoned up a warmly polite smile and stepped forward to meet them.

"Good afternoon, Uncle. I hope you had a good trip."

Jack restrained himself from shooting out a toe and making sure Simon did just that.

They shook hands.

Jack gave himself eight out of ten for not scowling when he turned toward his cousin. "Whasssup, Simon?"

"Hello, coz... Was that supposed to be a word?" Simon glanced toward Uncle Avery, making sure he'd registered Jack's inappropriate greeting. "My my, don't you look spiffy."

"What are you doing here?" Jack asked. "Come for a

chance to look at Niagara Falls? Maybe try going over in a barrel?"

As usual, Simon's hand felt as limp as a raw piece of sole.

"No, I've set up a meeting with a potential new customer. A friend in the gold-mining industry gave me the tip-off—a merger that's just about to take place. You wouldn't have heard about it yet, I dare say."

"Sorry about that, old man." Uncle Avery's tone was bluff. "Thought I'd told you about Simon. Things slip my mind these days. Getting old, you know."

Jack took his elbow. "We both know your mind's as sharp as a steel trap. It's just that Simon is forgettable."

Uncle Avery pressed his lips together. Jack thought he saw a twinkle in his eye.

He jingled his keys. "If you don't mind waiting a few minutes, I'll go and get the Jag."

With his uncle and his enemy safely ensconced in the car, Jack set off for the city.

"Why are we bumping and grinding along like this?" Simon complained.

"It's from the winter. Freeze, thaw, all that doesn't do the road any good."

Ahead, Jack spotted a gaping pothole. Tempted to drive into it, just to spite Simon, he reminded himself the jolt wouldn't do Uncle Avery or the Jag any good. He gripped the steering wheel harder and tried to retrieve his earlier good mood.

"Welcome to Toronto," Jack said. "Otherwise known as Hogtown."

Simon's cynical drawl issued forth from the back seat. "No wonder it suits you so well, coz."

Jack, slowing to turn onto the highway, nearly

ground the gears. His teeth weren't quite so lucky. Consciously, he relaxed his jaw. He almost heard Freddi's voice, encouraging and soothing him. Suddenly he thought, why not? It would be easy to give her a quick call—pretend to check on the dinner reservation. He picked up his cell phone and hit the automatic dial.

"Hi there. Ahem. Just want to confirm, uh, the table."

"Everything all right, Jack?" Freddi asked on a giggle.

"Yeah."

"I'll be waiting up for you."

"Great."

He pressed the end button and stowed the phone.

For some reason the atmosphere in the car had turned frosty.

"You shouldn't talk on your mobile when you're driving, Jack," Uncle Avery said. "It's dangerous."

"What's more, it's illegal," Simon piped up from the back seat.

Jack did a shoulder check and swung into the fast lane. "Not in Canada, it's not. At least, not in Ontario. I don't know about the rest of the provinces." He'd better change the subject, raise the topic of conversation the English were famous for. "So, what was the weather like when you left?"

Uncle Avery waxed lyrical about the spring, the daffodils in bloom in his garden. He then went on to talk about the state of the British economy and told Jack what he thought of Tony Blair. Soon they were drawing up in front of the grand entrance to the hotel.

Dinner was a quiet affair, with just Jack and Uncle

Avery. Simon had excused himself, saying he had a headache from the plane and intended to go straight to bed. Jack was relieved.

Back at the hotel, he asked, "What time are we meeting tomorrow?"

"Come for breakfast at...shall we say seven? I'm sure to wake up early seeing as we'll still be on London time. Then we can go to the office and get down to business."

Jack agreed, although he felt a pang of regret. If he had to get up at six, there'd be no lengthy canoodling with Freddi.

BY THE TIME Jack got home there wasn't much left of the night, too little to tell Freddi all about the evening and Simon's unexpected appearance. Happy to find her asleep in his bed, he gathered her into his arms, nuzzled into her neck and before long he was living his favorite dream fantasy.

In the morning, Jack woke just before six. Rolling over, he regarded Freddi. She lay there, his butler, his lady, so sweet and lovely, he couldn't bear to wake her. Even if she was bare, all delightfully, temptingly naked. Moving quietly so as not to disturb her, he got out of bed and headed for the bathroom. Still warm from their intimacy, he felt ready to cope with the day, strut his stuff and impress the hell out of Uncle Avery.

FREDDI STOOD in the dining room, carefully examining the beautifully arrayed table set for three. She'd picked up Jack's message to add a third place when she'd got back from a short walk in the warmth of the spring afternoon.

Now she was occupied with a different form of exercise, mentally running over her arrangements for the dinner. Everything was in place. She wouldn't let Jack down tonight, although she did wonder who the third person might be. Maybe Uncle Avery had brought Aunt Tina with him.

That could work well for Jack. Freddi couldn't imagine any female not being won over by him. He'd impress his uncle and get his heart's desire. Over the short time she'd been here, she'd learned how much it meant to Jack to be able to launch his new company. She'd do everything in the world to help him.

Tonight Freddi felt radiant, glowing with well-being. Her entire body was satisfied. Jack's lovemaking had been thrilling and thorough. She knew that she should be feeling guilty, that she'd broken the most important, number-one rule in the book. But boy, did she feel good. As if she'd just received a new infusion of life. Maybe she was finally putting Simon's demeaning treatment behind her at last. Thanks to Jack and this job, her self-esteem quotient was on the up.

Time to check on how things were going in the kitchen.

She opened the oven to look at the beef Wellington. Uncle Avery was sure to be impressed. The first course of asparagus lay cleverly arranged on the octagonal plates, tied up with slim strips of raw carrot and celery. Everything was in order.

She heard the sound of the lock and the door opening. Quickly untying her apron, she hung it on the hook behind the door and stepped out of the kitchen. Familiar voices sounded in her ears, a familiar figure met her eyes. That slim shape, that dirty-blond hair...that rat! Simon!

Gasping, she retreated, almost falling over her clod-hopping feet in their heavy lace-ups in her effort to make herself scarce. Far from going forward to help Jack at the door, she wanted to die, disappear, dive down the plug hole.

Jack looked around, puzzled. He was no good at hanging up overcoats and such. Where was his butler? Why wasn't she here to smile at him, bolster him with some reassurance?

"Come through, guys," he invited, forgetting to use a more formal form of address. "What can I offer you to drink?"

Still no sign of Freddi. Where was the woman?

Jack poured drinks and sat down to chat with his uncle, doing his best not to entirely exclude Simon, knowing that rudeness wouldn't help his cause.

Simon, his attitude of bored sophistication well in place, was finding demeaning things to say about Jack's house.

"Rather odd, having a staircase right there, almost in the center of this empty space, isn't it? And why do the spiral thing? You should think of putting a pond at the bottom. Then you could get some goldfish to swim around. They'd provide some interest at least. Haven't you heard of feng shui?"

"Is that the term for the bad smell under your nose?" Jack countered.

Puzzled at Freddi's nonappearance, he at last went into the kitchen to check that she was there. Sure enough, she waited by the stove. He thought she looked a little pale. Sliding an arm around her waist, he gave her a quick squeeze.

"Why've you been hiding, Fred? We should eat soon."

Freddi swallowed. "I know. Everything's ready. I just—"

"Fine. Then let's go for it."

And he disappeared before she could say another word.

Oh Lord, now she was in for it. How she wished for a disguise. Clapping the colander on her head wouldn't help much.

Chairs scraped on the hardwood floor. The diners were taking their seats. Time for her to present the first course. She hefted the tray with its plates of asparagus, straightened her shoulders, lifted her chin and went out to meet her doom.

14

UNCLE AVERY SHOWED no sign of recognizing her, although one bushy gray eyebrow twitched. Bless him. How many Saturday afternoons had she and Tabby spent happily at his and Aunt Tina's home in Gloucestershire when they'd had time off from the exclusive ladies' college they attended? The couple had never had any children of their own, and delighted in entertaining the two young girls.

And, wonder of wonders, Simon didn't seem to register her presence. He was more interested in checking out the food on the plate she set before him and trying to squint a glimpse of the label on the wine waiting on the sideboard.

Freddi was grateful for even that small reprieve, and gratified to note that Jack was behaving beautifully. A surge of pride rose in her. How very distinguished he looked tonight. No one would suspect he'd prefer to be dressed in his ripped T-shirt and track pants rather than the finely tailored suit he wore so well. If she survived the evening, she'd be able to congratulate him with complete sincerity.

Starting with Uncle Avery, who sat at the head of the table, she poured the wine, doing her best to be as discreet and unobtrusive as possible. But the gnawing nerves in her stomach made her hands tremble. Aware of Jack's gaze on her, she caught his eye after making a small loop to serve Simon. Jack winked. Distracted, she tipped the bottle. As she did so, she felt Simon's hand stroke her rear end. Her arm jerked, causing the stream of liquid to lose its aim. Wine trickled down the edge of the glass and splashed onto the cloth.

"Idiot." Simon's tone was only slightly censorious. His action had been automatic.

But Jack, seated opposite, must have seen what happened. He leaped to his feet, his expression thunderous. Simon smelled danger and swung around, sending his wineglass flying. He jumped up to avoid getting a lapful of wine and his chair fell backward. Freddi reached to save it, turning away just in time. Simon hadn't recognized her...yet.

Jack rounded the table in three strides and seized Simon by the lapels of his jacket.

"Keep your filthy hands to yourself."

Uncle Avery intervened. "Jack. Simon. Sit down, both of you. Enough of this reprehensible behavior."

Jack released his cousin.

Simon, always ready to be polite as well as to make trouble and show Jack up, stretched a hand down to help Freddi to her feet. She had no option but to comply.

His bland expression changed to one of astonishment.

"Oh, hello, Freddi old stick." He put his hands on her shoulders. "What are you doing here?"

Jack didn't seem to have heard the words, but he definitely saw the action. A look of blind fury came over his face. Instead of returning to his seat, he stepped closer, pushed out his chin and glared at Simon.

"Hands off, you nasty slug."

"It's no business of yours, Jack." Simon's tone was firm, but he let her go. Freddi stepped aside.

"That's just exactly what it is," Jack said. "Business of mine." And he swept his right arm back.

Without thinking, Freddi curled herself sideways to seize his fist or wrist, but she was hampered by the wine bottle that she still clutched in her hands.

Too late. Jack had already thrown the punch. However, her diversionary movement proved enough to deflect the blow. Jack's fist caught Simon on the ear instead of the chin.

"Boys, boys! Enough of this childish behavior." Uncle Avery might as well have saved his breath. Neither of them took the slightest notice of him or his outrage.

"Ow! Damn you, Jack. That hurt."

"Good. You deserved it."

Holding his hand over his ear, Simon transferred his attention to Freddi.

"I had no idea... I thought you were still in Paris."

Jack froze. Freddi gripped the wine bottle closer to her breast.

Simon looked from Freddi to Jack and back to Freddi again. He narrowed his eyes.

"You *know* her?" Jack fumed, his eyebrows snapping together.

"Of course," Simon replied airily. "We were engaged."

Freddi closed her eyes in despair. Wasn't that just like the snake, to make as much trouble as he possibly could? Obviously he was determined to get Jack rattled enough to revert to more uncivilized behavior.

"You're a bloody liar," Jack accused.

"Jack! That's quite enough. And watch your language!" Uncle Avery admonished.

With a quick glance at a scowling, smoldering Jack, Freddi stepped away so that she was out of Simon's reach and no longer between the two men. In an effort to reestablish her role and retrieve something of her dignity, she placed the wine bottle on the sideboard and straightened her jacket.

Jack shot Freddi a searching look. "Is this true? You're Simon's fiancée?"

She swallowed, nodded, and opened her mouth to explain. "Ex," she bleated. "We *were* engaged, but no more."

But already he was retreating, as if he hadn't heard. No longer looking at her, he went back to his place. "I see."

She'd never heard him sound so icy, so cold, so distant.

He sneered at Simon, who sank back in his seat with a satisfied air. Rolling his shoulders back in an elaborate shrug, Jack glanced at Uncle Avery, then said, "I apologize. Apparently I was acting under a misapprehension."

White-faced, Freddi stood gripping the back of a chair. She stared at the ruined table setting. The stain had spread, and if she didn't remove the cloth soon, the damp would leave a water mark on Jack's beautiful oak table.

"Please excuse me," she said, and stepped forward. "If you gentlemen wouldn't mind holding up your wineglasses."

With bemused expressions, they complied with her request, watching as she neatly set aside plates, glasses and cutlery, then transferred them to the sideboard.

The table cleared, she folded the sides of the cloth inward and removed it.

"It'll only take me a moment to set things to rights," she murmured.

But how long would it take her to set matters with Jack to rights?

With the tablecloth bundled in front of her and a sick feeling in her stomach, she headed for the kitchen. After stashing the cloth in one corner, she opened a drawer and took out what she needed. Then she returned to the dining room.

"Now, if you wouldn't mind, I'll replace the cloth with mats." She matched her actions to her words. "The beef Wellington is ready to be served... Would you do the carving, Mr. Carlisle?"

Uncle Avery got up, obviously thinking she was referring to him, although she had intended this to be an opportunity for Jack to show off his carving skills. She disappeared into the kitchen to fetch the vegetable dishes.

Jack followed her.

Arms stretched sideways and up, he grasped the door frame, leaning into the kitchen, looking dangerous and blocking her escape.

"A fiancé? Odd that you forgot to mention one before we hopped into bed."

She stared at him and opened her mouth to reply.

Uncle Avery's head appeared behind Jack, framed in the angle of his elbow. "I say, shall I carve all the beef Napoleon?"

"Not Napoleon, sir, those are the pastries."

He looked doubtful, then winked at her. "Glad to see my nephew's met his Waterloo."

He disappeared. The question was, which nephew was that?

Jack straightened, folding his arms, but still glowering at her. She'd wanted this chance, and here it was. Unfortunately, in the face of his cold fury, not one suitably clear thought or word of defense occurred to her.

"Why didn't you tell me about you and Simon?" Jack's voice was deceptively soft.

There was Uncle Avery's wavy gray head again, bobbing just above Jack's left arm.

"You didn't say... Shall I carve *all* the beef Nelson?"

Freddi closed her eyes and switched her mind to catering matters. "No, about half will be fine."

She transferred her attention back to Jack and took a deep breath in. This time the words came out in a rush. "Because my past had nothing to do with this job."

"Hadn't it?" Sparks of icy anger darted from his eyes. "You didn't think it relevant to tell me you're engaged to him? Not even when I asked you directly whether or not you knew him? Not even after..."

She shook her head. Then she lifted her chin and spoke emphatically. "We're not engaged. I broke it off." She twisted the dish towel through her fingers. "That's why I came to Canada."

She thought he was about to question her further, when Uncle Avery appeared yet again, this time to give her a brief update.

"I've finished the carving, m'dear."

"Fine, thank you. I'll bring out the vegetables now." She found she couldn't move.

Uncle Avery's voice issued from the dining area.

"Jack!" He sounded imperious. "Come back here and sit down. I would like to finish this excellent dinner and I can't do that without the presence of my host."

"We'll talk later," Jack said through clenched teeth.

Her senses reeling, her emotions in a turmoil of confusion, upset and dismay, Freddi carried the loaded tray through and set it on the sideboard. Only her own considerable self-discipline got her through the process of dishing out the food and presenting it with suitable ceremony and aplomb. She felt as if she was carrying out the motions under hypnosis, so little did the scene seem real. At last the men were served and she could retire. She was more than ready to leave them glowering at one another, although Uncle Avery seemed to be quite happy, applying himself to cleaning up every morsel on his plate.

When she felt sure they must be finished the main course, she went back into the dining room.

The men fell silent when she entered. With trembling fingers she collected the large plates. Under pretense of grasping his napkin, Uncle Avery gave her hand a quick squeeze. That made the tears prick her eyes and caused a catch in her throat.

Simon got up, all plummy tones and false cordiality. "Let me help."

"No, thank you, Mr. Sherbourne. Please, sit down. I think you've done enough."

She cast a quick glance in Jack's direction. He sat, both elbows on the table, quaffing back his wine. He raised an enigmatic eyebrow at her and spoke.

"She doesn't need help. She's a model of efficiency. That's Elliott."

She didn't like that cutting tone. It carved right into her.

"I'll bring in the pavlova," she said.

"You've got a ballet dancer hidden in the kitchen?" Uncle Avery perked up again. "Jolly good show."

"No. It's the pudding."

In the kitchen, she placed the individual portions of meringue and fruit onto dainty dessert dishes and loaded them onto the tray. Simon appeared and tried to take it from her.

"Get out, Simon. I told you, I don't need your help."

He held up his hands, as if to humor her, and began to retreat. "All right, all right."

This time Uncle Avery cleared his throat and spoke into the silence that greeted her. "We should make our plans for tomorrow," he began. "Shall we do more of the same? The three of us can meet for breakfast and go on to the office, Jack."

Jack fired a look at Freddi, as if suspicious as to what had been going on in the kitchen.

He tossed back a mouthful of wine. "That'll be fine, Uncle Avery."

Coffee and liqueurs didn't do much to relieve the tense atmosphere at the dinner table. Freddi only hoped poor Uncle Avery wasn't left with a bad case of indigestion. As for Jack, she was very much afraid the time of reckoning would soon be upon her. She'd never experienced this side of him, and realized with a pang how she missed his habitual teasing manner.

Even though the house was as warm as ever, she began to feel cold, filled with dread about the coming confrontation.

15

JACK KNEW he was in no state to drive his uncle and cousin back to the hotel. Apart from the more-than-usual amount of liquor he'd imbibed, the emotions roiling inside him were likely to cloud his vision with fury. In short, they wouldn't make for safety, so he called for a cab.

Within ten minutes he and Freddi were alone in the house. Anger, hurt and jealousy mingled in his gut, creating an unpleasant miasma of letdown and disillusion. His body felt as if he'd taken a beating. But worst of all was the feeling of betrayal.

He went to the kitchen where Freddi was in the last throes of cleaning up. She had stacked the piles of plates on the counter and was busy putting them in the cupboard. Leaning in the doorway, he watched her. As usual, she looked neat, tidy and buttoned up. Except for her shoes. Her feet must be tired, because she'd taken off the lace-ups and was now in her stocking feet. He remembered those stockings. Lacy-topped black stockings must be one of the biggest turn-ons in the world. For him, Freddi had been the biggest turn-on in the world. But all along, the whole time, she'd been two-timing him. It didn't matter that she said it was over with Simon, it still was betrayal.

She seemed determined not to look at him. A crazy

concoction of feelings welled up in him. Accusatory words rose, hiding his heart's cry of pain.

"How could you do this to me, Freddi? Didn't your conscience worry you at all?" His crushing disappointment turned to anger. He felt like sweeping an arm along the counter and pushing the piles of plates onto the floor, breaking everything, just the way she'd broken everything they'd had together.

She stilled and turned to face him. "You mean, about Simon and me? I saw no reason for you to find out or to know."

"So, if Simon himself hadn't arrived here, you would have merrily gone on spying for him, feeding him secrets about my business, is that it?" Jack shook his head. "Good old Simon, always the snake in the grass. I just wasn't expecting you to be slithering right along with him."

Looking stunned, she stared at him as if she had no idea what he was talking about. Up till now, he hadn't realized what a good act she could put on.

"Spying? For Simon?" she echoed. "Why?"

He noticed she appeared paler than before. Almost as white as that expensive porcelain dinner service she'd bought for him.

"Because that's how Simon operates and I have no idea how you still feel about him. Yeah. I see it now. He decided he'd nab my idea and get going in Europe while I'm still starting up in North America."

"Wait a minute!" He saw her sway. "Is that what you believe? That I would spy on you?" Two spots of color appeared on her cheeks and she narrowed her eyes. "For Simon?"

A crisp nod. "Clearly. That was why you were so insistent on getting into my computer."

Her eyes were round now. "So that's what you think of me. That I have no principles, no loyalty... That I would behave like—like a female version of your precious cousin."

"He's not my *precious* cousin, as you put it. He's your precious fiancé."

"No, he's not! I told you, I broke it off! Why won't you believe me? Haven't you come to know me at all in the weeks I've been here?" Her voice broke.

Oh yes. He'd come to know her. All too well. He took another kick to his gut, remembering.

"Fine." Reaching behind her, she untied her apron and cast it aside. "Then maybe it's time for me to do what you wanted me to from the word go."

He saw her draw herself up and switch into her butler role. He moved through to the dining room. She followed.

"With immediate effect, I resign."

"You can't do that." Even through his disgust, a kind of panic seized him at the thought of her going. He caught up with her at the bottom of the stairs and seized her wrist.

"Your contract says you have to give forty-eight hours' notice."

"You're going to hold me to that?"

"Yup. Business is business. Isn't that right, *Elliott?*"

He saw her throat move. She looked down at his hand and shook her arm. He let her go.

"Right, then." Her voice was tight. "I'll work two more days." She started up the steps.

The words whirled in his mind, accompanied by

flashing images. He watched her black stocking-clad calves disappear up the stairs, and felt a headache coming on. And a hangover.

AFTER A RESTLESS NIGHT, during which she'd lain awake, alternating between fury at Jack's injustice and grief over lost dreams, she'd finally fallen fast asleep in the early dawn. The loud ringing of her alarm clock might have been a lullaby, so little did it penetrate her consciousness. When she woke at last the house was quiet. Jack was long gone.

Moving slowly, as if her joints ached, she went downstairs. All the harsh words, the ugly drama and accusations hung in the air, ready and waiting to smother her. No. She straightened her shoulders and went to open some windows. This too she'd live through. If Jack knew her so little, had so little insight into her true nature that he believed she'd be so dastardly, then it was best that this whole episode was about to end. Two more days, then she'd board a plane to London and leave Jack Carlisle and his stupid, blind, suspicious nature far behind. Tabby would find her another job.

Freddi decided to take a walk along Acorn Street.

How hard it was to think of leaving. Somehow, living there with Jack, running the household, had made her feel this was her home. She'd been looking forward to seeing the avenue of maples come out in leaf, the crab apples in the park in blossom. But now these surroundings, for her, would always remain like this— poised on the brink of spring.

She stumbled along, catching her tears with a tissue.

One or two passersby glanced at her curiously, but she managed to hold back the threatening flood.

By the time she reached Yonge Street she had herself under control again. She waltzed into salsa class. Exercise would help.

An hour later, sweaty but restored, she felt able to face her problems. Walking back, she began scheming. First of all, she'd need somewhere to live in London. Now that she could afford to pay rent again, the best thing would be to go and live in her own flat. She'd notify the tenant who'd taken on the sublet right away.

Once in the house, she climbed the stairs to the office to see if she could find a suitable flight on the Internet. She scanned the possibilities and it didn't take long before she found what she was looking for.

THAT MORNING, Jack was relieved his cousin wouldn't be around, poking his finely chiseled nose into his business. So far Uncle Avery had appeared interested and impressed with everything they'd gone over. But, arriving early at the hotel to pick him up, Jack was very much afraid he'd blown the whole deal. If nothing else, Simon had sabotaged his chance to prove that he had acquired all those social refinements, skills and graces he'd been lacking. Although Jack didn't feel the least regret at having punched his cousin, he was prepared to do damage control.

His uncle sat at a small table in the hotel café/restaurant, eating a piece of toast with marmalade and drinking tea. Jack pulled out the chair opposite and sat down.

"Good morning, Uncle Avery."

His mouth full of toast, his uncle nodded.

Jack went on. "I must apologize for last night."

His uncle finished swallowing, and looked at him from under stern, gray eyebrows. "You behaved badly, Jack."

"I know." From the sober tone, it sounded as if he was in for a grilling.

"Somehow, up till the time you attacked Simon, I had thought your manners greatly improved."

"Thank you," Jack replied stiffly. "I admit…well, I didn't exactly treat him as a guest should be treated."

"No, that's true." With his knife, Uncle Avery prised a large dollop of shiny orange marmalade out of the miniature glass jar. Obviously he'd never had an Elliott telling him he should use a spoon. Jack watched in silence as he spread the conserve liberally on the triangle of toast. Then the need for self-justification rose in him.

"But I couldn't let him insult Freddi—er—Elliott, like that."

"Quite right, m'boy," said Uncle Avery as he waved the piece of toast around. Jack could just hear Freddi telling him he shouldn't do that. "My thought was that you mostly behaved appropriately… In fact, I can't remember when last I had such an entertaining evening. Particularly as Simon got exactly what he deserved."

Jack caught the twinkle in Uncle Avery's eye. "You think so?"

"Oh, yes."

He gave a chuckle. At least, that was how Jack interpreted the rumble in his throat.

"You should have seen his face when you clipped him on the ear. Sheer outrage and disbelief!" He bit off a large mouthful and crunched. "I would have tackled him myself if my age weren't so much of a handicap."

Surprised at Uncle Avery's approval, Jack sat back, folded his arms and grinned. "I bet those muscles of yours are still strong."

"Could be worse." Uncle Avery took a long slurp of tea. "Seems to me," he said in a thoughtful tone, "life suits you here in North America. Huge market potential, you know. And with that touch of polish you've acquired from Fre...er...Elliott, I think you'd function well in Europe...provided, of course, you rein in your tendency to passion and violence. Although, I daresay the Italians would understand that...and also the French, for that matter."

Jack stared. He'd never heard Uncle Avery wax so lyrical.

Uncle Avery went on. "It's interesting to see how my nephews are shaping up. My niece, too. Tabitha is proving herself to be a very competent business-woman."

Not sure where all this was going, Jack nodded slowly. "Sure. She's definitely got what it takes...in spite of having sent me a female butler instead of a male."

Uncle Avery didn't look at all astonished to hear that. "Might have been intentional."

Jack could feel the way his raised eyebrows stretched the skin on his eyelids. He lowered them. "Nah. Must have been a slipup."

"Has it been so bad?" Uncle Avery demolished the last of the toast and tea. "Having a female butler, I mean. She looked pretty efficient to me."

"Yep, pretty and efficient, that's Freddi."

"Ahem." Uncle Avery shifted on his chair and set his crumpled napkin on the table. "Let's get going."

Feeling somewhat cheered, Jack drove to the office. They soon set to work. However, after a few hours he began to register the downside of Simon's absence. He was on the loose. The question was, what was the bastard up to today?

Jack decided he'd had enough. All this emotional sweating wasn't healthy. Time to do something about it.

"Uncle Avery, you're looking a bit tired. Why don't I take you back to the hotel for a rest? We'll get together for dinner."

His uncle carefully wound down his gold Parker ball-point pen and closed his leather folder. "A good idea. These old bones of mine still haven't adjusted to the time change."

Jack decided to leave the Jag parked in the hotel for the meantime and catch the subway home—he had no desire to tackle rush-hour traffic.

Before bidding him goodbye, Uncle Avery looked at him piercingly and said, "There are a couple of questions to which I'd like you to give serious consideration. First, I want to know if you could see yourself as head of Quaxel and living in England. Second, if not, who would you see as a good person to take over from me?"

Jack opened his mouth to reply, but Uncle Avery stalled him by holding up a hand.

"No, don't answer me now. We'll talk in a week or two. I'll have had time to think things over myself by then."

At first Jack took the two questions to be a positive sign. Then he realized they could just as easily mean Uncle Avery was letting him down gently, hinting that

Jack would not be named to the top post. Surely he wasn't seriously considering Simon? If he wasn't chosen, at least he could concentrate all his efforts on his new business venture.

Jack climbed the station stairs two at a time and emerged on Yonge Street. The day was bright, but a chill wind blew from the north, lifting the flaps of his suit jacket and making his blue-striped shirt flutter close to his skin. He shoved his hands into his pockets, hunched his shoulders and headed for Acorn Street.

The slim, familiar figure of another man, a tasseled scarf casually flung over one shoulder, walked in front of him. No specter this time, but Simon himself.

Rage and frustration bubbled up in Jack, a passionate tide that shut down his thought processes and made his blood boil. This guy was the cause of many of his troubles. He'd destroyed all the fun of the past weeks and put Jack's future in jeopardy.

Involuntarily, Jack's legs picked up speed. He strode ahead and found himself directly behind his cousin. Without considering his actions, he seized Simon's wrist and hoisted it up toward his shoulder blades. He held his cousin trapped in a satisfying half nelson. Take that, you scheming little Napoleon.

"Hey!" Simon squirmed and twisted in panic. He looked over his shoulder, saw Jack and relaxed. "Oh, it's you. What do you think you're doing, coz? This is hardly appropriate behavior."

"Don't talk to me about appropriate behavior." Jack twisted and hoisted a little harder and higher. "That's the only thing that's stopping me from really hurting you."

Being slight of build, Simon was at his mercy. Jack's grip on him tightened and he turned his cousin to face him.

He sneered, but Jack could see a trace of genuine concern flicker in his eyes. "Jack! Don't be infantile!"

"I've got a score to settle with you."

Simon held his ground, glaring up into Jack's eyes. "No, you haven't. Since last night, we're quits."

"Oh yeah? What about setting Freddi to spy on me— my own butler, my trusted, right-hand woman? We haven't begun to factor that one in yet."

Jack increased the pressure. The half nelson gave him immense satisfaction.

"Freddi? Spy on you?" Simon's eyes bulged. "You must be mad. My advice to you is to follow the North American fashion. Go and consult a psychiatrist."

Jack squeezed just a little more. "Are you telling me the truth? She wasn't spying for you?"

"Hey! Ease up, won't you? I can assure you it was a complete surprise to find her here, waiting on you."

Suddenly Jack was hit by an awareness of what he was doing. Hell and damnation, once again Simon had provoked him to violence. What was going on in his head? Perhaps his cousin was right, he was crazy. Letting his hands fall to his sides, he took two steps back. He pictured Simon's face when he'd first registered Freddi's presence. Maybe he *was* telling the truth.

Simon adjusted his cuffs and brushed off the sleeves of his blazer. But Jack wasn't quite finished with him yet.

"What are you doing, heading to my house?" he demanded.

"I'm on my way to join you for dinner, of course."

Right. Uncle Avery was sure to expect Simon to accompany them tonight.

"Okay. But if you don't want a repetition of these recent incidents, can I suggest you get lost for a while? We can meet at the hotel in a couple of hours—where we're supposed to meet anyway."

Simon's eyebrows rose. "I see. You *think* you're going to make everything right with Freddi."

Battling the urge to seize him again, Jack folded his arms. "I doubt it."

"It's unfortunate for you that she's leaving." Simon sighed and looked wistful. "She was the best thing that ever happened to me."

Jack watched his cousin adjust the knot of his tie, smooth his hair and set off in the direction of the subway.

Now to have it out with Freddi. His thoughts and emotions were so mixed up he had no idea what he was going to say to her.

Inside the hallway, he took off his dark glasses and hitched them over the nose of the marble bust.

Freddi appeared, ready to help him off with his coat. What a pity she couldn't remove his blinkers as easily.

Jack walked toward her, but he was still distant. "I'm sorry. It seems I probably made a false accusation last night."

Although that sounded like a conditional apology to her, a small bud of hope began to unfold.

"Which one was that?"

"The business about spying for Simon."

The hurt, the resentment, cramped in her heart, a hard, tight knot in her chest. Even a sincere-sounding apology would probably not be enough to unravel it.

She picked up an egg-shaped stone from the console table and turned it over in her hand.

She looked at Jack. "Why did you change your mind?"

"Simon told me the truth."

"What a miracle. How did you make him do that?"

"I got violent with him."

"I see... How was that different from when I told you?"

Jack was silent. At last he said, "I guess I believed you in the logical part of my brain, but my gut was twisted over the whole thing. I needed confirmation."

Freddi waited expectantly, but soon realized that that was all he was going to say. There would be no rapprochement, no tender scene of reconciliation. Her tiny, last, pathetic remnant of hope died. If he was so blind to her needs, to her feelings, then she had her answer. Her decision to leave was the right one.

Her throat began to close, thick with tears. Any moment now they would overflow. She certainly wasn't going to cry in front of Jack. All she had left was her dignity. She turned away and walked to the stairs, clutching the banister to give her support as, step by step, she spiraled her way upward. Blindly she felt her way down the passage and into her room.

RETREATING TO THE KITCHEN, Jack went to the fridge and poured himself some iced water. A piece of cheese would be good, too. And he had plenty to choose from. Freddi had him very well stocked, ready to cater to any whim. She'd provided everything and anything that might take his fancy, including his favorite Busha

Browne's hot relish. How she'd discovered that addiction, he didn't know.

Jack stood sipping his water, staring at the neatly arranged shelves, the cheese forgotten. Freddi had done wonders on the practical level—she'd supplied him with food, organized his clothes and laid them out for him every morning. She'd prepared an itinerary for him, downloaded his e-mails and got rid of the spam. She'd stocked his cellar with excellent wines, and poured them for him when he dined; fixed up his car, kept his living spaces alive with lovely vases of bright flowers. She'd instructed and encouraged him. She'd shined his shoes...

But that wasn't the whole of it, nor even the most important. Freddi had brought a zing to his life, a special ingredient that had to do solely with who she was.

In twenty-four hours she'd be gone.

What was Freddi doing upstairs in her room? Suddenly he had to know. Abandoning his glass, he closed the fridge and headed for the second floor.

The door to the spare room stared blankly at him. Freddi had shut him out. Knowing he was breaking the rules of politeness, Jack seized the handle and barged right in. He stopped, taken aback by the sight that met his eyes. A strange emotion trickled through him when he realized what she was doing.

She was packing.

16

"GETTING A JUMP on things in your usual efficient manner?"

Freddi didn't look at him, but kept lifting garments off the pile on the bed and dropping them into the suitcase.

She answered in a dull voice. "No. I'm leaving tonight."

With a kind of detached interest, Jack noted that the jumbled effect she was creating was quite different from the meticulous layers of the bag she'd packed for him.

Her words ricocheted in his mind. He couldn't believe she was leaving. No matter how mixed up he felt, how furious, he knew one thing for certain. He wasn't ready to let her go.

"What about the forty-eight hours?" he asked belligerently.

Freddi kept her head down, doing her best not to look at him. "Everything's well organized. You won't need me." All she wanted to do now was to get away. "The taxi to take me to the airport will be here soon. Would you mind listening for the bell?" she asked.

"Of course I mind. You can't go. Your job's not over yet."

"I think it is."

Freddi looked directly at him. There he stood, so

handsome, so stupid, so blind, so lost to her. She
looked down again. It would be awful if he realized
how devastated she felt. Hopefully the room was shad-
owy enough that he hadn't noticed her puffy eyes.

"There's nothing more I can do for you. And it's important I get back."

Freddi counted five heartbeats before his response.

"Why?"

"I've got another job lined up," she lied.

"So quickly? Mind if I ask what you'll be doing?" He
leaned against the wall, folding his arms.

"It's—uh—working for a pop star."

"Oh yeah?" A dark eyebrow quirked. "Who could
that be? I wonder."

"I'm not allowed to say." Freddi let her gaze slide
away from those glinting eyes. "That was the very
strict precondition."

Into the suitcase went the last bundle of clothing.

"Your uncle hasn't said anything yet?" she asked.

"Only that he's reserving judgment."

Freddi batted the lid of the suitcase. She heard it
close with a sharp snap. Or maybe that was her heart,
beginning to crack.

A minute or two went by before he spoke again.

"That's all you're taking? I seem to remember a certain low mountain range of luggage that first night
when you arrived."

Both of them were quiet, remembering.

"It's all packed and downstairs by the door."

Jack unfolded his arms. "So you're really going
back." Back to London and her life without him. Probably she'd never give him another thought. But he'd
certainly remember her.

"Looks like it, doesn't it?" She smoothed the bed, getting rid of the impress of the suitcase, leaving no sign of her occupancy.

"I'll drive you to the airport, if you like." Then he'd have just a little longer to be with her.

"No thanks. I don't need you to do that."

Okay. He got the message. Clearly he didn't feature in her plans or her future.

The doorbell sounded. Jack sighed and wondered why the chimes made him think of a death knell. He hefted her suitcase and wrestled it down the spiral stairs. She followed him.

Outside, the cabdriver heaved her luggage into the trunk. Jack held the rear passenger door open for her and watched her climb into the back seat. He shut the door.

She half unwound the window.

"And let me know—you know—how everything turns out," she said, her big dark eyes gazing up at him.

He nodded, doing his best to imprint her image on his memory.

The cabdriver banged the trunk and got behind the wheel. The engine growled, and he pulled out into the road.

Freddi turned back toward Jack, and gave a sad little wave.

That was that. She'd better go. He'd do fine without her, he was sure.

Somehow the thought gave him the strangest, hollowest feeling deep in his gut. He watched the cab disappear down the road. When it was gone, he turned and trudged up the steps to his empty house.

A WEEK LATER, Freddi sat on the upper deck of a red London bus. She looked down at the Oxford Street traffic and thought about the loss of her beloved old Mini Minor. Taking public transport certainly eased the acute city parking problem, but it also took up a lot more time.

She hopped off the bus and opened her umbrella. At the beginning of May, the British Isles still waited for a hint of summer. Huddled under the black silk canopy, the rain a gray mist in front of her, she hurried down South Molton Street toward the small Georgian terrace house where the buttling agency had its offices.

Reaching the aubergine-painted door, Freddi closed her umbrella, and shook off as much of the rain as she could. In the tiny lobby, she leaned the umbrella in the corner and climbed up the narrow staircase.

"'Morning, Freddi," Polly greeted with forced brightness.

Muttering a response, Freddi dripped past the front desk into Tabby's cluttered office and found her friend working at her desk. Tabby's hair was more mink brown than sandy blond like Simon's. Although she had a firmer chin and rounder features, there was a faint resemblance to her brother. Today she looked businesslike yet feminine in an ankle-length navy skirt and soft cream blouse.

Freddi shrugged out of her raincoat. "It's chucking it down out there," she complained.

Tabby stopped frowning at the paper she held and drew off her tortoiseshell-framed glasses. Leaning to one side, she pressed the button on her intercom. "Coffee for two, please, Polly."

"I see the parrot is as chirpy as ever."

"Polly's not so bad. You shouldn't be so resentful. I've never known you to hang on to a grudge for so long." Tabby pointed at her with the earpiece of her glasses. "You know, Freddi, you should actually be grateful to her friend."

Freddi made a rueful grimace. "Yeah. If it hadn't been for her pal Sharon, maybe I wouldn't have woken up to the fact that Simon could never be faithful to me."

Tabitha nodded. "I love my brother, but I'm aware he's not ideal husband material. You're well out of it."

"It's true." Freddi sighed. Over at the sash window, she leaned her hands on the sill. "I don't know why I'm so crabby these days. It must be the weather... I mean, look outside—" she indicated the sky with her chin "—nothing but gray, gray, gray. We're supposed to be enjoying spring sunshine."

Polly came in, gingerly carrying a small tray. She set it down on one corner of Tabitha's desk.

Freddi felt ashamed of herself. "I'm sorry I was unfriendly when I came in."

"Oh," Polly said, perking up. "That's all right, Freddi."

Wobbling a little on her ultrahigh heels, she tottered out.

Tabitha handed Freddi a yellow coffee mug. "A trip to Brazil might do the trick."

"It's winter there now." Freddi set her mug on the corner table and flopped down onto the brown leather armchair. "I don't think my dreaded budget would approve."

"I don't know about that." Tabitha lifted some papers on her desk as if she was looking for something. "I have something for you. From Jack."

Freddi's heart leaped. "A letter? An e-mail? What I would *really* adore just at this moment is a big bunch of roses."

Tabby stood up and came toward Freddi, an envelope in her hand. "No. Something more useful."

Freddi's spirits sank again.

"Take a look in there. The contents might brighten your day." She settled in the armchair's twin, at right angles to Freddi.

Again, hopes and dreams rose up and drifted through Freddi. Maybe Jack had sent a plane ticket. The paper crackled as she tore off the end and peeked inside. Not a plane ticket. A check. With trembling fingers she withdrew the printed form. Her mouth fell open when she saw the amount.

"Tabby! This is insane." Her eyes fixed on the bold signature.

"Is it?" Her friend regarded her with a slightly curious expression. "I don't know. Obviously Jack put a high value on your services. He said to say this is the bonus he promised you."

Suddenly warm, Freddi fanned herself with the envelope. "I didn't expect him to be so generous."

"That's Jack for you."

"Jack for me," she echoed. Then blinked when she realized what she'd said. "Did he mention anything else? In the note, I mean."

"Nothing." Tabby leaned one elbow on the wide arm of the chair. "What went on between you two, Freddi? You never really told me about the last few days."

"I know, Tabs." She bit her lip and gazed into the depths of her coffee mug. "It hurts too much to talk about it."

Tabitha seemed to be waiting to hear more, but Freddi couldn't bring herself to elaborate. At last, swallowing the lump in her throat, she found a way to shift the emphasis.

"Any news of how things are in Toronto? I presume the check means that Jack got his money from Uncle Avery."

"No, he didn't."

"What?" Freddi sat up with a jerk and spilled a splash of brown liquid on her black skirt. "Damn."

"As far as I know, Uncle Avery's still shilly-shallying. And he still hasn't decided on his replacement, either."

"That's unlike him."

"It is and it isn't. I can't help feeling the old chap's got something else in mind...but who knows?"

Both Freddi and Tabby sipped their coffee, silent for a while. Freddi battled against the pangs of heartache that crushed her every time she thought of Jack and their weeks together. How many times had she relived this incident or that conversation, remembering how Jack had looked, how he'd moved, how he'd spoken or laughed? And then there was the wonderful way he'd made love to her, the way she'd felt when he kissed her.

She swallowed. The past was past. It was high time she got on with her life. The trouble was, she wasn't having a whole lot of success in that direction.

"And now, about my next assignment." Freddi spoke firmly. "Please tell me you've got something worthwhile for me. If the money is this good, I wouldn't mind doing another job for you."

"Well, er..."

Freddi clapped her hands over her ears. "Don't say it! I don't want to hear about it if it's the sash-presentation evening of the Esteemed Order of Nudists or the Bicentennial Bash of the Doomsday Soothsayers. I know you have some odd jobs! I just wish you'd find me a big event to organize, something beyond buttling maybe."

"Now, now, don't be impatient. I'm on the lookout. I know these kinds of jobs don't offer you a chance to put your talents and skills to good use, but at least it's work."

Freddi heaved a sigh. "I suppose. Looks like I might as well go back to secretarial work in the meantime, but that's not exactly a step forward."

"Don't do that yet. I'll go through the new requests myself, and let you know on Friday when you come to dinner."

JACK SAT at his home-office desk. He pushed himself away from the computer and ran his fingers through his hair. Damn. He had no idea what he'd done with that urgent phone message he'd scribbled on a handy piece of paper. Maybe it had gotten mixed up in the pile of mail downstairs, the pile that would soon qualify as a mountain if he didn't sort through it in the very near future. Now, if Freddi had been around, everything would be organized.

Why hadn't he realized sooner what a jewel she was? If only he could talk to her one more time, confess what a fool he'd been, tell her how he missed her. But she was incommunicado, working for that cursed pop singer. It might be spring, but life was looking as bleak as February.

If Freddi had been around, the house would feel different. Knowing he'd see her when he went downstairs, he'd have that zing of expectation. Maybe he'd be planning to waylay her in the kitchen or dining room, or even in the entrance with old Julie looking on—if the marble bust could see anything through those blank eyes of his. She'd be busy in the kitchen, her head bent forward so that the lovely nape of her neck, so creamy against the dark brown of her hair, was revealed. Bending forward, he'd gently put his lips—

The hell with fantasizing. He had to take a transatlantic trip. Go find Freddi.

The phone chirped. "Carlisle."

"How's my favorite cousin today?"

"Good, thanks, Tabby."

"What, no opportunities to be bad?"

"Not so far."

"My sympathies. I just phoned to ask if you got the stiffie."

"Huh?" She couldn't possibly mean what he thought she meant.

"From Uncle Avery."

"Huh?"

"You know, a stiffie—the classy, high-society kind with a deckled edge."

"Deckled?"

"Yeah, sort of frilly."

Jack looked down at his lap. "I don't know whether or not mine's classy, but it definitely isn't frilly... And,

Tab, not even in my weirdest dreams could Uncle Avery ever give me a stiffie."

Gurgles issued from the earpiece. Jack smiled.

"Glad to be entertaining, especially on your dime."

"Okay. Well, I'm talking about Uncle Avery's invitation—you know, a stiff piece of card as opposed to a floppy one."

"Yeah, right."

"You must have got it in the post by now. I'm dying to know what you're going to do about it."

"No idea. Is it important?"

"I think so. It's his 70th birthday party, but my hunch is that the shindig's going to be significant for us all."

"Hmm. I was just thinking I'd have to go and sort through my mail. Probably the invite's buried somewhere in that mound."

"When you've finished your dig, give me a call."

Downstairs, Jack picked up one load of various-size envelopes and shiny flyers and dumped the whole pile on the dining table. Most of this junk would go straight into the recycling box, but somewhere in there were the two communications he needed.

The invitation proved fairly easy to locate. Interested to find out just what Tabby was referring to, Jack tore open the envelope and began to read. The black letters set his mind to scheming. This could provide him with a way to find his missing lady. He wondered where she was, and what she was doing at that very minute.

FREDDI WAS IN Tabitha's chintzy, feminine bedroom. After a leisurely dinner, the two women had left Richard to smoke a cigarette on his own in the garden.

"Still feeling blue, are you?" Tabby finished reapplying her lipstick and looked at Freddi in the mirror.

"You saved me this evening." Freddi leaned back on the bed. "But, yeah, most of the time I'm into the deep, dark Prussian."

Tabby turned to face her. "Are you sure that's not due to a tall, dark Canadian?"

"Yes. No. I mean." Freddi gazed at the ceiling, determined not to cry. "I'm not sure at all. Anyhow, it's over. I don't expect I'll ever see Jack again."

"Hmm. That's really up to you."

"No, Tabs. I can't go back."

"You won't need to. He's coming here."

Freddi jerked upright. She stared at her friend.

"Uncle Avery's invited everyone to a banquet, a big do for the family and the firm." Tabby's diamond bracelet sparkled as she waved one hand. "That's sure to be when he'll announce his retirement and his successor. Jack's coming over for the occasion."

Freddi jumped to her feet, hope surging through her.

"Both rivals are required to take 'suitable' partners with them," Tabby continued. "Jack specially asked me to contact you."

Freddi's spirits rose.

"He'd like you to organize a date for him."

Freddi's spirits sank.

She began pacing, twisting her fingers in front of her. "Jack and dates...that's a recipe for disaster. Uncle Avery would *hate* the kind of woman Jack considers desirable." She paused and looked at her friend. "Simon's going to take Sharon with him, is he?"

"Don't be ridiculous," Tabby answered. "He's about two or three women along since then—at least, that I know of. From what I gather from the parents, he's got his sights on Caroline Steele.''

"Oh yeah. That should put him on the cutting edge.''

"Freddi...'' Tabitha sounded exasperated. "Will you stop that!''

Freddi sank onto the bed again. "Sorry, Tabs.'' She sighed. "I just don't know what's wrong with me these days. Perhaps you're right. Maybe I do need to take a holiday.''

Her gaze shifted to the bay window. Blobs of gray and white clouds hung heavy in the sky. She knew she'd been moping around like a lovesick cow. Lovesick. Oh boy.

"You spoke to Jack on the phone, did you?'' she asked Tabitha.

"Yes.''

"Did he say he was missing me? How did he sound?''

Tabitha gave her a meaningful glance. "Miserable. But you know what men are like...closemouthed as clams.''

Freddi's heart gave a kick. Was it possible that Jack was missing her, yearning for her too? Tabitha stood up and went to sit next to Freddi on the bed, putting an arm around her shoulders.

"Why don't *you* go with Jack? We both know Uncle Avery thinks the world of you.''

Freddi stared at her friend. "You seem awfully keen to get us together again.''

"*Moi?* Why would you think that?''

"Because I know you well, Tabs. And, come to think of it, it strikes me the whole thing smells of a setup.''

Tabitha's next words diverted her from examining

her growing suspicions. "Well, anyway, unless you want Simon to be named as Uncle Avery's successor..."

Freddi shook her head. "We should do something to sabotage his chances."

"Good idea," Tabitha added. "Copy his devious mind and we're sure to come up with something."

"Hmm. Talking of devious minds, I'm wondering if it's genetic."

"You mean?"

"Did you perhaps send me to Toronto with a bit of matchmaking in mind?"

Tabitha looked embarrassed. "Guilty as charged. Both of you mean a lot to me. I was hoping that if I told Jack to keep his hands off of you, he'd be sure to do the exact opposite."

Freddi sighed. "For a very little while, that's what happened."

"So what are you going to do?" Tabitha asked before Freddi could sink into the morbs again.

She thought about that. Men could be obtuse about admitting they were in love. Sometimes a woman had to fight for her man. And that's exactly what Freddi Elliott was going to do.

"I'll go with him. But promise me, Tabs, you won't let on. If it's a surprise, then maybe I—" she broke off and hitched in a breath "—maybe I'll find out if I mean anything at all to him."

17

TABITHA LEANED FORWARD and hit the office intercom. "Polly, come in here a minute, would you? We need your help."

Clearly surprised, Polly pranced into the office.

"Take a seat."

Freddi already occupied one of the armchairs. Polly came over and perched on the arm of the other.

"How would you like to attend a banquet?" Tabby began.

"At the Ritz. With Simon." Freddi added.

Polly shifted her skinny behind. The leather was slippery and, with a shush and a whoosh, she slid down and landed on the seat, her pale, thin arms flung out sideways, her legs akimbo.

"See," Tabby went on, "this is how it is. You know that Simon can be something of a louse, don't you?"

Polly sniffed. "Yeah."

"Here's your chance for a little revenge. He needs a partner, and we want it to be you. This banquet—it's going to be rather a grand affair. Because you already know him, well, you could hint that you're going to spill the beans about the way he treated your friend if he doesn't agree to invite you."

"I dunno."

Tabby slid one arm along the back of the chair so that

Polly had to turn her head and look up to her. "Didn't you tell me you were taking night classes in drama?"

Polly nodded.

"We'll need you to play a certain kind of character, one that won't get approval from my stuffy Uncle Avery, who's giving the party. You can drape yourself all over Simon, bat your eyelids, kiss him on the dance floor, whatever takes your fancy."

Polly blinked at her. Slowly her expression brightened. "You want me to play a tart."

"Yes, Polly, we want you to be the Dreadful Date," Freddi confirmed with glee, and explained the plan she and Tabitha had cooked up together.

As soon as Polly left, Freddi settled back into the armchair.

"Talking about the banquet is making me nervous. Oh God, Tabs—what on earth am I going to wear?"

"Something stunning, of course."

"Stunning costs money. You know I'm trying to be frugal."

"In this case, a little extravagance could pay dividends."

"I'm not good at shopping for those kind of clothes. Funky's my thing, not glamorous."

"Wish I could help you, but I'm snowed under." Tabitha indicated her cluttered desk. "Do your best—it'll be fun."

To FREDDI'S SURPRISE, Tabitha turned out to be right. The dress she bought was floor-length, a shiny, satiny creation in deep rose, with a V neck low enough to show some cleavage. A folded draped effect gathered into a twist at her waist and unwound over the A-line

skirt, giving the effect of an overdress, and revealing
the shape of one gently curved hip. It was perfect, and
well worth every penny.

FREDDI'S TAXI surged up out of the underpass into Piccadilly and drew level with another black cab. Tonight
she'd drawn the one taxi driver in the whole of London
who had ambitions to race at Brand's Hatch, but now
the traffic had stymied him. Idly she gazed out the side
window and into the window of the parallel vehicle.

A bubble of powder-blue hair caught her eye. She
looked closer and saw Polly's snub-nosed profile,
fetchingly embellished with a diamond stud. Freddi
tried to peer inside to gauge Simon's expression. She'd
love to see him fuming, curls of steam coming out of
his ears. But she was foiled by the fact that he sat back
in the shadows of the far corner of the taxi. When the
traffic began inching forward again, she glanced at her
watch. Seven minutes to seven. Her heart fluttered.

Leaning forward, she spoke through the glass partition. "Do you think you could get me there by seven?"

"O'course, love. Don' worry about a fing."

Her taxi driver accomplished a dexterous maneuver
and accelerated, leaving the cab containing Polly and
Simon behind, still stuck in the gridlock.

Freddi stroked one hand up over her elbow-length
gloves and touched her fingers to one earring and then
the other. With a movement that mimicked the jumping pulse of Freddi's heart, the taxi jerked forward. At
two minutes after seven, Stirling Moss drew up at the
Rue de Rivoli–style arches that marked the facade of
the hotel.

After paying the fare, she climbed out, smoothed

down the billow of her wide skirt and lifted her chin. Then, with a quick breath in, she stepped toward the foyer and the evening that would determine her destiny.

18

As SHE ENTERED the foyer of the hotel, Freddi's eyes swept the stately space and found him immediately. Jack Carlisle. Her love. A thrill moved through her. He stood with his back to her, handing his key to the desk clerk. In the black fabric of his dinner jacket his shoulders looked wider, straighter than ever, and that errant wave in his dark hair glistened in the light of the wall sconces and overhead chandelier. As if he felt her eyes on him, he turned and looked at her.

The kick to her gut was swift. God, he was handsome.

He was also five minutes late.

As soon as she spotted a slightly askew, Las Vegas–style bow tie in place of correct, formal neckwear, she knew exactly what had held him up. And now her heart was doing a tricky thing, melting and tap-dancing at the same time.

For a few seconds Jack stood staring at her, one hand in the pocket of his trousers so that his dinner jacket hitched up on one side. But at last he drew his hand out of his pocket and came forward. Feeling like Eliza Doolittle in *My Fair Lady*, Freddi held out one slim, long-gloved arm. She saw his throat bob as he swallowed, and then he grasped her outstretched hand.

"How have you been?" Jack's voice sounded gruff, quite unlike his normal baritone.

Freddi had no chance to answer, because Tabby hastened forward to greet her cousin. She kissed Jack's cheek. "So, you're finally back in the U.K."

"Yes. Uck."

"I know, the weather. And I agree."

"Come on." Tabby switched to her best boss tone. "They're waiting for us to take our seats at the high table."

Jack's gaze fastened on Freddi. He was totally bowled over by this fragile, fairylike creature of beauty. He cleared his throat.

"Freddi, I'm—"

Tabby cut him off. "—dazzled. I know. It's the chandeliers. They have the same effect on me."

Richard gave a snort. He exchanged a man-to-man commiserating glance with Jack and clapped him on the shoulder.

"Sorry, old chap. Can't keep the old bugger waiting."

Jack turned to look at Freddi and asked, "Am I to assume I've been set up?"

"You have, Mr. Carlisle. I hope you approve of the choice for a date," Freddi replied with a warm smile.

"Couldn't be better."

Jack crooked his arm invitingly and Freddi hooked her hand under his elbow. Her fingers pressed into his sleeve. A feeling of relief, a lifting of his spirits spread through him. With Freddi by his side he could conquer the world.

Freddi tugged at his arm and cocked her head. Her shaggily straight hair emphasized her thickly lashed, sparkling eyes.

Tabby gave him a little shove. "Into the fray we go."

Stepping forward, his cousin gave the footman their names.

"Mr. and Mrs. Richard James," he announced.

Jack felt Freddi curl her fingers around his arm. Lifting her chin, she indicated the open doors of the banquet hall. Her fancy earrings danced and dangled. Jack had an urge to nibble them aside.

"Shall we?" she said.

He wished. Especially when she looked so very delectable.

Jack and Freddi stepped up to the double doors.

"Lady Frederica Etherington-Elliott and Mr. John Carlisle."

Jack stared down at her. "That's you? Your full name?"

He'd known she must come from a snooty background, but he'd never expected this. Like a tornado hitting, all his doubts, his feelings of social inadequacy caught him up and spun him around.

He felt her take a step forward, and as he did the same, his cell phone banged against his hip. It reminded him of business, and that pulled him out of his funk. What did it matter if he was plain Jack from London, Ontario? He could still be her hero. He would offer her something bright with promise, a life not hidebound nor restricted by out-of-date social conventions. If he pulled off this new deal he'd be able to lay the world at her feet.

Freddi, distracted by the feel of his hand on her upper arm, the warmth of his body radiating against hers, answered his question about her full name, "Er, not quite."

"Give."

She drew in a deep breath and spoke it all out as fast as she could. "Lady Frederica Imogen Etherington-Elliott." Pressing her lips together, she smiled ruefully at him.

"Fi." Jack stretched one foot out in front of him, wiggling it from side to side. "And to think you shined my shoes."

Unspoken was what else had happened between them. Jack's hand sought hers. Fingers linked, they walked into the hall.

Long tables, beautifully decorated, stretched the length of the ballroom. Fellow guests, mostly employees and their spouses, were already assembling. As they took their places, they exchanged greetings with friends and co-workers, settling in to celebrate the seventieth birthday of the founder of the firm.

Once Jack and Freddi were seated at the table, they hardly had the opportunity to exchange more than two words. People kept coming up to greet Jack. Freddi was interested to see that he was obviously well liked. In addition, he didn't seem nervous at all, unlike herself.

Simon, on the other hand, was as wound up as a toy mouse. He dodged here and there, apparently doing his best to buttonhole his uncle. No doubt to explain his choice of girlfriend. How he'd do that, Freddi couldn't imagine.

The old man himself was in top form, full of bluff good humor and cordiality. He wandered around, ducking Simon and his attempts at self-promotion, greeting people, paying compliments to the ladies. But at last he sat down and Tina soon joined him.

"How is everything in Toronto? Are Kimmie and Louise doing well?" asked Freddi.

Jack turned toward her. His knee brushed hers. Was that deliberate or by chance?

"Pretty good, on both counts. Louise said to tell you you'd better come visit soon."

Freddi's laugh came out sounding wistful. "Ah well," she said vaguely, "that won't be possible for a while."

How difficult it was to behave normally when she was as attracted to him as she was. If she gave in to her body's urges, she'd be crawling into his lap right this minute. Just as well that the first course had been served.

From time to time, Freddi cast surreptitious glances in Jack's direction, wanting to be sure he was managing okay. He caught her once, and sent her a cheeky wink. But she needn't have been concerned, because his manners were impeccable. He hardly hesitated over which fork to use. And he correctly divided his attention between politely chatting to Tabby and attending to Freddi with a warm solicitousness she'd only witnessed once before, when he'd baby-sat Kimmie.

The entrée had been served and eaten. Jack looked at his watch and pushed back his chair. He nodded first in Tabby's then in Freddi's direction.

"Please excuse me for a few moments."

Without waiting for a response, he got up and left.

Minutes passed. Freddi thought he'd return at any moment, but when the dessert was served, then cleared, she began to be concerned. Anxiously, she looked around the ballroom. Where on earth was Jack? He'd been gone over half an hour now, and she knew that Uncle Avery had noticed. Sick at heart, she watched the clock, conscious of the minutes ticking by.

"All on your own, my dear?" Uncle Avery took a seat next to her. "What's happened to my nephew?"

"I believe he—er—went outside for a breath of air."

"I can't imagine that the pollution from the traffic on Piccadilly's going to help much. He shouldn't have left you alone."

Just what she'd been thinking.

"He's sure to reappear at any moment."

"Hmmph. Time to return to my seat. Maybe you'd better go and bring that nephew of mine back inside."

Another couple of long minutes went by. Freddi gathered her skirt around her and stood up to go and find him. Her dress swishing as she walked, she sashayed out into the foyer.

There he was, talking to the desk clerk. She caught up with him just as he turned away.

"Where have you been?" she asked anxiously. "Don't you know it's a mistake to leave the field of battle for too long?"

"I had to take a call. Promising news about some business—"

"Yes, but Uncle Avery—"

"...can go fish. What matters is this."

Caught in the depths of his gaze, she read his intention. Little chills shivered through her. Her lips parted to allow her quickening breath to escape. Without so much as another heartbeat's pause, Jack drew her into his arms and took her mouth. His kiss was deep, soul-drenching, so perfect for her, so drugging to her senses that the surroundings faded away. She was wrapped in his arms, back in the wonder of him. No one could be better than this, no one else could ever taste like this, unique and yet so marvelously familiar. Her love.

She became aware of a funny noise, buzzing, insisting on her attention... It was the desk clerk, clearing his throat.

"Ahem."

She realized where they were and pushed at his shoulders.

"Jack, no! We can't behave like this in public."

His lips moved against hers. "Yes, we can."

Jack felt like hoisting her over his shoulder and heading for a room instead of attending a stuffy banquet. To compensate, he took her lips again, drawing her into that place where they were together, where no one else mattered or existed.

Freddi moved in closer...and felt something hard against her thigh. Something man-made. An appliance.

She wrenched her mouth away. "Jack, what have you got in your pocket?" she asked.

Reluctantly, Jack lifted his head. He pressed his lips together, but the corners of his mouth twitched.

"It's my cell phone."

"Your mobile? Is it turned on?"

He cleared his throat unnecessarily. "I believe so."

She bit her lip. "You'll have to switch it off."

He'd already told himself that a time or two, but he hadn't been referring to the phone.

"I'm expecting an important call. When it comes I'll have to run off."

She was thinking about his phone and paid little attention to the second sentence. "Haven't you got voice mail? Couldn't you leave a message?"

He thought about that. "Yup. Okay. I'll say I can be contacted through reception."

A glance at his watch told him there was still a while to go before he could expect to hear the final verdict.

"Actually," Freddi continued, "the best thing would be to leave the mobile at the desk. Uncle Avery loathes the things." Her eyes dropped and rose again. "And—" she swallowed "—you don't want the weight to harm the drape of your trousers."

"Oh, no, can't have that. But it's not the phone that's causing the problem."

Freddi gave a gurgle of laughter and saw Tabby burst through the double doors. She came bustling up to them.

"Jack! Freddi! The speeches are about to begin and soon Uncle Avery's going to make The Big Announcement. He's looking like thunder every time he sees your empty places. Come quickly."

In the center of the main table sat Uncle Avery and Aunt Tina. Next to him on one side were Tabitha and Richard. Freddi and Jack took their places next to them. On the other side, Simon had been placed next to Aunt Tina.

Polly, Freddi observed, was putting on a sterling performance. She tittered, draped herself over Simon and lolled back in her chair. Either she was a much better actor than Freddi had suspected or she was already buzzing, and heading fast to being seriously intoxicated.

At last Uncle Avery stood up to talk. He adjusted the lapels of his dinner jacket and cleared his throat.

"As many of you know, I have chosen the occasion of this, my seventieth birthday, to announce my imminent retirement." He surveyed the room, making eye contact with people here and there. "Yes, it's high time I moved out of the way and allowed fresh, younger blood to take over the task of leading into the future. When I look back over all the years at Quaxel, how I started as the proverbial messenger boy, riding my bicycle to deliver letters—"

Tabby leaned over the table and whispered to Freddi, "Lot of lying rot."

"—going to the bank, and slowly working my way up and learning the business, I have to say I think the modern way is better. Get your MBA and go straight into management."

Simon gave a smirk and wiggled his shoulders.

"Nevertheless, making a success of your life by overcoming odds of education and background, may I even say, location, is also an admirable accomplishment."

At this obvious reference to Jack, Tabby gave him a thumbs-up.

"In all aspects of life today, and especially in business, it's vital to move with the spirit of the times."

Polly yawned and flopped her head down onto the table.

Uncle Avery sent her a surprised look, then continued.

"Quaxel is a family company and we want this tradition to continue. So I have looked to my close relatives for a successor."

Simon, ignoring the prostrate Polly, stretched his neck and preened like a peacock.

Uncle Avery pulled his glasses down his nose and looked over them at the gathering. He cleared his throat and took a breath.

"Now I realize you are all eager to know who I'm going to appoint to take over from me. Possibly, my decision will come as a surprise. This has not been an easy choice to make, especially as I didn't want to step down until I was certain I would be doing the right thing."

He reached down, picked up his glass of water and took a sip. "However, after much consultation and rumination, I am now ready to present to you my successor."

Simon pushed himself a little away from the table, obviously preparing for the moment when he would leap to his feet and make an acceptance speech. His confident air made Freddi want to choke.

Jack, on the other hand, wore a polite expression. He looked relaxed.

Uncle Avery went on. "This person has already been tested and proven in the world of business and, in spite of being still of a comparatively young age, has demonstrated vision appropriate to the spirit of entrepreneurship."

He turned toward the younger generation seated on his right and held out a hand in their direction. In a commanding tone he proclaimed, "My niece, Mrs. Tabitha James."

19

FOR FIVE FULL, long seconds, the hush held. It was Jack who broke the silence. He lifted his hands and began to clap, loudly and enthusiastically. Spatters of applause came from here and there until the whole room erupted. One or two people cheered.

Tabitha sat blinking in surprise. Then a smile lifted the corners of her mouth, replacing her stunned expression.

Freddi hardly dared to look at Jack, hating the thought of what this would mean to him, even though it would be absolutely marvelous for Tabby. She saw Richard reach for his wife's hand and link his fingers through hers. A pang of envy hit her, a small stab to her heart. That was what it was to have a companion in life, someone by your side, always *on* your side, always wanting the best for you, yet willing to share the defeats as well as the triumphs. She couldn't help wishing that she and Jack could set out on such a journey together.

Poor, darling Jack—how terrible he must be feeling! Gathering her skirt in her hands, she shifted toward him, ready to offer comfort and sympathetic support.

He reached for her hand and gave her fingers a quick squeeze, his attention on Tabitha. "Way to go, coz."

Tabitha gasped. "I must be dreaming!" She clapped

one hand to her cheek and shook her head. "I can't believe it!"

Jack glanced across at Simon. His cousin had flopped back in his chair. A dull red flush of anger stained his cheeks.

Uncle Avery picked up his wineglass, raised it high and faced right, center and left. "Here's to the future, to a new era for Quaxel, and to our new managing director—Tabitha James."

All other interchanges were put on hold while the toast was drunk. Chinks of glass against glass, the murmured endorsements of all the other guests following suit, rustled through the room.

Freddi felt a pat on her shoulder, but a *ting ting* demanded her attention.

Nodding and smiling, Uncle Avery tapped a fork against his glass. "Now it's time to celebrate my birthday. I hope you all enjoy the party... See you on the dance floor."

He sat down to a prolonged round of applause.

Freddi turned toward Jack. He was no longer by her side. Instead, he was making his way to the crowd around his uncle. She sighed. Maybe they'd have a chance to talk when he came to ask her for a dance. Surely that would be soon.

"Time to kick up our heels," Richard said to Tabitha, helping his wife to her feet.

Freddi grabbed her friend by the elbow, eager to offer congratulations before Richard swirled her into a waltz. "Tabs!"

Flushed with pleasure and pride, Tabitha opened her arms. They embraced, kissing each other on the cheek.

"This is a turn up for the books, isn't it?" Tabby's eyes shone. "Who would have thought Uncle Avery would ever even consider a woman as his successor?"

"I'm sure you'll do a wonderful job."

"Thanks, Freddi."

Freddi turned away, intending to go and find Jack. But there at her side, plump cheeks smiling, double chin wobbling, stood Aunt Tina.

"Come and sit next to me for a few minutes, Freddi dear. I'm dying to hear all about Toronto and your version of that ridiculous dinner party."

Freddi itched to excuse herself, but she couldn't put off Tina. The times that she and Tabby had visited Aunt Tina and Uncle Avery had been precious, a much-appreciated respite from the routine of boarding school. Promising herself she wouldn't be long, she sat down next to the older woman. Out of the corner of her eye she saw a tall, dark figure disappearing through the door, followed by one of the liveried hotel employees. Jack. Resigning herself to putting him out of her mind, if not her emotions, for a little while, she began chatting. Aunt Tina's few minutes turned into half an hour.

While Freddi was congratulating Tabby, Jack went for a quick word with Uncle Avery.

"THAT WENT OFF all right, didn't you think, Jack?"

"Absolutely. Couldn't have been better."

"People were surprised, just as you predicted." Uncle Avery chuckled, and waved his unlit cigar in the direction of the dance floor. "I showed them there was life in the old dog yet."

"You did indeed."

Another guest claimed his uncle's attention. Jack escaped.

Now to ask Freddi for a dance. He was about to move in her direction, when he felt a tap on his shoulder. He jerked around. A liveried hotel employee waited to speak to him.

"An urgent phone call for you, Mr. Carlisle."

Aha, this was what he'd been waiting for. This would give him the news, inform him whether or not his funding was approved and his new company ready to fly. If there was an affirmative, he'd be able to offer Freddi her heart's desire. But he hadn't had a chance to explain things to her, and he really needed to do that. What must she be thinking? How had she taken Uncle Avery's announcement?

"Mr. Carlisle?" The man waited for a response.

Knowing Aunt Tina and the way she could talk, he guessed Freddi would be stuck for at least half an hour. The call shouldn't take more than a few minutes. He could duck out.

Jack gave a curt nod. "Thank you. I'll take it downstairs, not in my room."

He got up and strode off.

ANGUISHED MINUTES kept Freddi churning inside. It seemed like an hour before she sensed Aunt Tina was willing to let her go.

"I'd better get back," she said.

"Ah, yes. No doubt my nephew's waiting for you." Aunt Tina patted her on the arm. "Make sure you give the handsome devil a good run for his money."

Remembering the bonus, Freddi decided she'd already done that. She swished back to her place, but the neighboring chair was empty.

Where was Jack? She scanned the dancers. No sign of her tall, dark lover. How strange. There was Polly, her pastel-blue head tucked into the hollow between Simon's shoulder and his neck as they swayed to a slow, romantic ballad. Simon didn't seem to mind too much—not at all, in fact.

Surely Jack hadn't gone off to drown his sorrows? Of course, he could be paying a visit to the men's room. She'd wait a while.

Another half hour went by. Puzzled, she sat, idly watching the dancing. Tabitha caught her eye and headed her way.

"You look like you're waiting for someone," Tabitha said.

"Well, I want to find Jack, actually."

"I think I saw him leave."

She thought back. Jack himself had told her he was waiting for an important phone call, and then...and then he'd said he'd have to run off. Now he was nowhere to be seen.

All the life seemed to drain out of her body. She felt completely empty. A minute ago the world had been so full of promise. And Jack had kissed her! He couldn't have gone off, just like that, uncaring, without a word, not even a goodbye.

"Maybe he's still in his room... Why don't you run and see?" comforted Tabitha.

Sick at heart, barely holding on to herself, Freddi threaded her way through the milling guests. She looked around the now almost deserted foyer. No sign of Jack. When she rang up to his room, there was no reply. She asked at the desk.

"Mr. Carlisle, madam?" The clerk looked left and right. "He was here, but he's gone."

That was her last hope. It must be true. He really had left.

She drifted back toward the banquet hall and stood on the threshold, feeling her life was in ruins. All these people, dancing, laughing, drinking, enjoying themselves. She couldn't possibly go back in to the party.

Blindly, she stepped outside. Arms crossed, hugging herself, she stood looking out through one of the stone archways at Piccadilly. Rain poured down, a wet curtain of misery.

"Taxi, miss?" the doorman asked.

She was about to shake her head, when she thought, why not? So, instead, she drew in a breath, swallowed and said, "Thank you."

Within moments she was climbing into the black interior.

"Where to, miss?" the driver inquired.

She gave him her Hampstead address.

Tears slid down her cheeks. She fumbled in her tiny evening bag and found a lace-edged handkerchief, one of several she'd kept from her mother's things, one that should have brought her luck.

But hadn't.

20

BACK AT THE RITZ, Jack was in the best of spirits. He couldn't wait to tell Freddi of his triumph. As he crossed the floor, heading for his seat, he did a quick soft-shoe shuffle.

Apart from his uncle, there was no one sitting at the high table. Many of the guests had already left. He must have been away longer than he'd anticipated.

Uncle Avery, cigar between two fingers, waved at him.

"Come over here, Jack. Want a word with you."

Obligingly, Jack went to sit next to him.

"Good that you were here...kept Simon in check. Sometimes I despair of that nephew of mine."

"Maybe this will teach him a lesson."

"Let's hope so, but I doubt it." Uncle Avery took a long draw, put his head back and puffed out the smoke. "He needs to stand on his own two feet and not someone else's. Wish I could force him to do that, but one way or another he always seems to land with his bum in the butter... Freddi was much too good for him, you know."

Jack's hand went to his bow tie to check if it was straight. "And what about me?"

"You?" Bushy eyebrows rose and piercing eyes looked at him.

"Do you think she's much too good for me? I was

kinda hoping, with this new venture of mine, that I'd be able to measure up."

"You do, Jack." Uncle Avery made a circling gesture with the cigar. "In my opinion, you certainly do. But I'd say the lady has to decide for herself. Better follow her and pop the question."

"Follow her?" Jack echoed. "Has she left?"

"All the young went off to a nightclub. Quaglino's, I believe."

Jack jumped to his feet. He was surprised she hadn't waited for him, had gone off without a word.

"Sorry about the funding. Your request came at a bad moment. I couldn't convince the board to take the chance. Good luck, m'boy." Uncle Avery grasped his hand and gave it a hearty shake.

Jack wasn't sure why, but he had a horrible feeling he was going to need it.

OUTSIDE, the liveried doorman asked, "Taxi, sir?"

"Yeah. Please."

But he had forgotten where he was going. The name had sounded something like Quaxel, only longer.

"Qua...qua..." he tried, pacing up and down the sidewalk.

"You quacked, sir?"

"Only trying to remember what this nightclub is called. Must be close by. Qua-something."

"Ah, Quaglino's."

"That's it."

Sure enough, after a short ride, he found Tabitha and Richard, Simon and Polly drinking cocktails at a small table.

Tabby looked up as he approached.

"Hello, Jack. Where's Freddi? Have you lost her?"

"God, I hope not. I thought she was with you."

"No," Tabby said. "She couldn't find you, so I told her to try your room. She must be frantic wondering where you are! Go and find her," Tabitha advised. "She's sure to be at her flat."

"Not at the pop star's?"

"No. There *is* no pop star." Tabby began scribbling on a piece of paper. "Here's her address and phone number. And hurry."

Within half an hour, he stood outside Freddi's apartment building. Next to the front door there was a vertical row of four doorbells and beside them the names of the tenants. Jack bent closer and squinted in the dark. Second up from the bottom he saw "F. I. Elliot." Okay, she was on the second floor. He stepped back and looked up at the expanse of the bay window. A light glowed. She was at home.

Back at the entrance, he jabbed at the doorbell, then bent to put his ear near the grill on the intercom. A crackle of static told him it had been activated, but no one spoke.

"Fred, darling, let me in. It's Jack," he said.

No reply.

"Please, my love, open the door."

Jack recoiled when he heard an annoyed, gruff male tone.

"No Fred here. What are you? Some kind of a nutter?"

Totally taken aback, Jack frowned. Had a thief broken into Freddi's apartment? He'd better check. Finger outstretched, he was poised to poke the doorbell again, when it struck him. In his agitation, he'd pressed the wrong button.

FREDDI HEARD the doorbell and huddled deeper into the corner of the couch. She wouldn't answer that. The thought of facing anyone was impossible. Whoever it was had better go away and leave her to her misery. She felt too raw now. Later she might have the courage to work things through so that, somehow or other, she could face a tomorrow without Jack. Brushing away a new surge of tears, she rested her head back and closed her eyes.

This should have been the happiest night of her life. For a little while everything had been perfect. The awful thing was, she didn't know what had gone wrong. Why had he left without saying goodbye? His careless disregard proved that he didn't care for her at all. How was she ever going to get over him? The heavy, desolate sensation in her heart, the ache of longing, was almost unbearable. A new tide of tears welled up.

She reached for a tissue, wiped them away and blew her nose. The prosaic action somehow brought her into herself. She'd be able to put herself together again and find the strength to go on. Somehow, she always managed.

After wiping her eyes again, she made a resolve. It would help to focus on something quite different. First thing on Monday she'd visit the travel agent. If her dream of a life with Jack was over, perhaps she could rekindle a long-forgotten dream of visiting Australia.

A grating sound, like grit hurled against glass, had her opening her eyes. Another blast. Whoever it was who'd rung her doorbell was now throwing stones at

her window! Slowly she got up, stepped over her discarded dress, which lay like a crumpled flower in the
middle of the floor, opened the curtain a crack and
looked down.

Jack stood below, on the dim, deserted street. He
could feel the wet seeping into his Italian leather shoes.
Rain trickled off his head and down his neck. At the
sight of Freddi standing with the light behind her, he
opened his mouth and shouted.

"Let me in, Fred, before I'm totally soaked."

The window on the floor above opened. A shaved
head craned out.

"Sod off before I call the fuzz."

Jack saw Freddi wave. Taking that for encouragement, he turned up the collar of his tux, hunched his
shoulders and began to squish back toward the entrance, thinking he might well start quacking.

He walked in, shucked off his wet shoes and took the
stairs two at a time. At the landing stood Freddi, and
his heart was full of love for her.

Another stride and he scooped her into his arms,
holding her tight, right against his heart.

"How could you think—" he began, his cheek
against her hair.

"Where did you—" She broke off at the sound of a
door being wrenched open.

"Oy." The voice wafting down the stairwell was all
too recognizable. "Let's have a bit of hush."

She gave a trembling smile, bit her lip and, taking his
hands in hers, drew him into the flat. Obligingly, Jack
followed. Once again he wrapped his arms around her.

"Oh Freddi, Freddi, I thought I'd lost you all over
again."

"I thought you'd gone," she mumbled, her head pressed against his chest, her arms around his waist.

Jack loosened the embrace so he could look down into her beloved face. "No, no. Just business I had to attend to."

Dark eyes gazed up at him. "I was so worried, wondering if you were terribly disappointed, how you were feeling."

"Now that I've found you, I feel great."

"But where did you disappear to? I couldn't find you. I tried your room, but you weren't there. The desk clerk said you'd gone."

"I was just along the hall...that phone call, remember?"

Freddi nodded and linked her arms around his neck. Jack gave her a tender kiss, then launched into the explanation. He'd worked things out with Uncle Avery beforehand and they'd agreed Jack would be better off staying where he was, establishing his new company. He told Freddi how he himself had suggested Tabby as the best one to take over as CEO.

"I thought about my father, and the business he founded in Canada, and I realized that's what I want to build on and where I want to stay. I'm hoping that will be okay with you. Would you be willing to put those great skills to use and help me with my new venture? Or do you love buttling? I'm not sure I could bear you doing all that for anyone else."

"I don't want to. I'd much rather be organizing. It was Tabby who pressed me into it. She had ulterior motives, you know."

"She did?"

"Yeah. I accused her of throwing us together. She admitted it."

"In that case, I owe her one."

She drew him into the living room. Once he was settled on the couch, she snuggled onto his lap.

"The good news is—" he smiled at her "—my phone call confirmed that I've got the funding."

"Congratulations!" She leaned forward to give him a kiss. He was more than willing to cooperate.

Too soon, he took his lips from hers. "Sorry, sweetheart, but there is bad news as well." He cleared his throat. "I do have to be back in Toronto tomorrow. I mean, today."

"Oh, Jack." She rested her forehead against his. "So little time to be together."

"Will you come with me?"

"I'd like nothing more."

Jack hugged her and then said, "Freddi, there's something else."

"What?"

"I'd like you to marry me."

"Marry me?" she squeaked, struggling to sit up.

"Ow! Careful or you'll damage the future generations." Shifting her to a more comfortable position, he looked at her with tender, smiling eyes. "I love you, Freddi. I think I must have fallen that moment you almost slid down my front stairs." He pecked her on the nose. "So, tell me, will you be mine? Will you marry me and live by my side?"

The efficient, always organized Freddi Elliott found she couldn't answer. Her throat was too choked up. Joy sang through her, swelling like a grand chorus in crescendo. Jack loved her. He wanted to marry her.

"Oh, Jack," she half giggled, half sobbed. "I love you."

"I love you too, Fred. But please, put me out of my misery and answer the question."

She let out a long sigh. "Yes, Jack, I will." Leaning forward, she nibbled on his ear. "What's more, I'll buy you a diamond."

"Hey! That's my line, not yours."

Her fingers played with his hair, curling at the ends from the rain. "I must warn you, we'll have to have a big society wedding."

"That's okay. I know all the snooty etiquette now."

His lady love squeezed his hand and leaned her head on his shoulder. "Brilliant. Also, there's the top hat thing."

"I can always donate that to old Julie afterward."

She slid down, smiling up at him in a very inviting manner. "You don't think he'd prefer my wedding veil?"

"Maybe he'd like to take turns. Since your visit, I think he likes being a cross-dresser," Jack murmured. Then he bent his head and kissed Freddi, taking all the time in the world to do it thoroughly.

Modern Romance™
...seduction and
passion guaranteed

Tender Romance™
...love affairs that
last a lifetime

Medical Romance™
...medical drama
on the pulse

Historical Romance™
...rich, vivid and
passionate

Sensual Romance™
...sassy, sexy and
seductive

Blaze Romance™
...the temperature's
rising

27 new titles every month.

Live the emotion

MILLS & BOON®

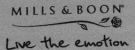

MILLS & BOON®

Live the emotion

Sensual Romance™

ROUGHING IT WITH RYAN by Jill Shalvis

South Village Singles

Gorgeous Ryan Alondo's life is overcrowded with responsibility, but he knows just how to alleviate some of the stress – an affair with fun-loving Suzanne. But she has vowed to forget about men and is determined not to fall for his charms. Good thing he can be very, very persuasive…

EVERYBODY'S HERO by Tracy Kelleher

When photographer Claire Marsden photographs hockey star Jason Doyle, it's not long before she persuades him into becoming a fake fiancé for her friend – but it's Claire he can't keep his hands off! Can he keep up the charade or will his secret desire be discovered…?

SOME LIKE IT SIZZLING by Jamie Sobrato

A half-naked man asleep in her bed isn't what Lucy Connors expected for her birthday. But soon she's shedding her conservative ways and letting Judd lead her to a sexy adults-only resort. When Judd Walker agreed to be Lucy's escort, he had no idea just how seductive she would be – and he's determined to prove to her that he's one gift she should keep!

HOT OFF THE PRESS by Nancy Warren *Sizzling™*

Reporter Tess Elliot is desperate for the chance to prove herself, but when the chance arrives she goes head to head with rival reporter and resident bad boy Mike Grundel, who's also out to get the scoop! Mike's sole interest doesn't lie in the job – getting under Tess's skin is just as fun – but it's getting her under the covers that's going to take some work!

On sale 3rd October 2003

Available at most branches of WHSmith, Tesco, Martins, Borders, Eason, Sainsbury's and all good paperback bookshops.

0903/21

Invitations to Seduction

THREE SIZZLING STORIES FROM TODAY'S HOTTEST WRITERS!

VICKI LEWIS THOMPSON
CARLY PHILLIPS · JANELLE DENISON

Available from 5th September 2003

Available at most branches of WH Smith,
Tesco, Martins, Borders, Eason, Sainsbury's
and all good paperback bookshops.

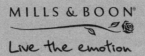

MILLS & BOON®

Live the emotion

Blaze Romance™

ABOUT THAT NIGHT *by Jeanie London*

Good girl Julienne Blake has decided she's going to be *bad*! With a bit of self-hypnosis, she'll unleash the passionate, sexy woman inside and experience the thrill of seducing a man with no strings attached. Her target is confirmed bachelor Nick Fairfax and he's instantly hooked. But is there more than just that one night between them?

THE ULTIMATE SEDUCTION
by Janelle Denison
HOT PURSUIT

Natalie Hastings won't give in to her attraction to private investigator Noah Sommers, even if it is mutual. Then an accident leaves her with short-term amnesia – and in danger – and the only way Noah can protect her is to convince her she's his fiancée. He's determined to keep his hands off until she can remember – only now *she's* determined to make him surrender! Can Noah resist the ultimate seduction?

On sale 3rd October 2003

Available at most branches of WHSmith, Tesco, Martins, Borders, Eason, Sainsbury's and all good paperback bookshops.

0903/14

FREE
2 BOOKS
AND A SURPRISE GIFT!

We would like to take this opportunity to thank you for reading this Mills & Boon® book by offering you the chance to take TWO more specially selected titles from the Sensual Romance™ series absolutely FREE! We're also making this offer to introduce you to the benefits of the Reader Service™—

★ FREE home delivery
★ FREE monthly Newsletter
★ FREE gifts and competitions
★ Exclusive Reader Service discount
★ Books available before they're in the shops

Accepting these FREE books and gift places you under no obligation to buy; you may cancel at any time, even after receiving your free shipment. Simply complete your details below and return the entire page to the address below. *You don't even need a stamp!*

YES! Please send me 2 free Sensual Romance™ books and a surprise gift. I understand that unless you hear from me, I will receive 4 superb new titles every month for just £2.60 each, postage and packing free. I am under no obligation to purchase any books and may cancel my subscription at any time. The free books and gift will be mine to keep in any case.

T3ZEC

Ms/Mrs/Miss/Mr ....Initials ....
BLOCK CAPITALS PLEASE

Surname ....

Address ....

....

....Postcode ....

Send this whole page to:
UK: FREEPOST CN81, Croydon, CR9 3WZ
EIRE: PO Box 4546, Kilcock, County Kildare (stamp required)

Offer valid in UK and Eire only and not available to current Reader Service subscribers to this series. We reserve the right to refuse an application and applicants must be aged 18 years or over. Only one application per household. Terms and prices subject to change without notice. Offer expires 31st December 2003. As a result of this application, you may receive offers from Harlequin Mills & Boon and other carefully selected companies. If you would prefer not to share in this opportunity please write to The Data Manager at the address above.

Mills & Boon® is a registered trademark owned by Harlequin Mills & Boon Limited.
Sensual Romance™ is a registered trademark used under licence.